BROKEN PUPPET

THE ELITE KINGS CLUB BOOK TWO

AMO JONES

PLAYLIST

Jason Derulo "Stupid Love"

The Weeknd "Or Nah"

Dead Prez "Hip Hop"

Avenged Sevenfold "Hail to the King"

Machine Gun Kelly "Bad Things"

The Game "It's Okay"

David Guetta "Where the Girls At"

Cheat Codes "No Promises"

Redman "Cisco Kid"

Cypress Hill "Tequila Sunrise"

Kendrick Lamar "Humble"

Tash Sultana "Jungle"

Tsar B "Escalate"

Tsar B "Myth"

DEDICATION

To the girls who have been through hell but come out with its fire burning through their soul, its crimson bleeding from their heart, and the devil as their side bitch.
This one's for you.
For us.
Straighten that crown.
Deuces.

PROLOGUE

M OMMY? I DUCKED BEHIND MY CLOSED BEDROOM
door.

As I peeked around the corner, my mom start-
ed raising her voice, stabbing her finger into the man standing
in front of her. "No, this wasn't part of the plan!"

The man smiled in a way that made me clutch my teddy,
Puppie, tighter. "You don't call the shots. She's a Venari. You
will have to run, and run fast if you don't want this catching up
with you."

My mom clutched the locket on her chest. "She…," my
mother whispered, tears slipping down her cheeks. "She's just a
kid, Lucan. She… she—"

"Is the Silver Swan, Elizabeth. You must run. Now, before
Hector finds out."

My mom sucked in a breath just as I stepped backward,

quietly running to my bed. Slipping under the covers, I wiggled into the warmth and clutched Puppie closer. It was my birth present from a close family friend, and I'd slept with her since. She had ballerina slippers, a loose dress, and her hands stuck up in the air when the puppet strings were attached. When my door finally cracked open, my eyes slammed shut as I began to scratch one of the button eyes on my teddy. The material was worn, and the puppet strings were now broken. I was seven though, so I should've been too old for Puppie to be sleeping in bed with me. But I know why the man was here.

He comes here every Friday.

I know what he does next.

Bleeding echoes reverberate around Madison's bedroom as sobs wrack through her body. Clutching her knees up to her chest, she scrunches her eyes closed, attempting to block out the familiar memories that assault her every night. Like a murky walk down a cold, damp road, alone, unable to break free from the confinement of which she's constricted to.

"This is part of who you are, Silver."

Goose bumps break out over her flesh at the slithering invasion of that voice. And then everything changes, as if she's watching herself from the outside as a different person.

"No!" Madison tossed and turned in his arms, attempting to break her wrists free from the tight grip strapped around her.

"Shhh, Silver, you're not your own."

"What?" Madison gasped, tears streaming down her cheeks. "What do you mean I'm not my own?" The hand that was around her wrists went to her loose ponytail, and he tugged it down slightly. "Please don't. Not tonight," Madison pleaded, her throat constricting through the pain, and the betrayal.

"You best get used to this, Silver. This is only the beginning *of your life."*

"But I'm little."

"This is better than being dead." Then he gripped onto Madison's pajama bottoms and tore them off, flicking them across the room. She closed her eyes and dreamed of a day, a better day, where her family secrets and ties weren't coming into her bedroom every Friday night. Black Friday was what Madison called it. She feared it, despised it, and one day, she hoped to put a bullet between its eyes. The first time, he stole her virginity. And Madison knew the blood that trickled down her innocent thighs wouldn't bleed without retribution.

CHAPTER I

"**M**ADISON? ARE YOU SURE YOU WANT TO leave?" Tatum asks, looking at me from over her arm, her hands resting on the steering wheel.

"Yes," I answer, gazing out the window. "I can't be around them right now, Tatum."

She looks at me, pulling onto the highway. "Do you want to talk about what happened back there?"

I hit the radio, hoping to drown out her questions. Jason Derulo's "Stupid Love" starts playing.

"So yup, that's a no then," Tatum mutters, taking her attention back to the road. I close my eyes and lose myself in the lyrics of the song. Fuck love. Fuck any feelings that resemble love, or show it. The one person who was supposed to love me unconditionally betrayed me too. What does that say? What, am I that unlovable? Or do so many people think I don't deserve their truth? Both of which are shit, if I'm being honest. Which I am.

The song finishes and I turn the radio down, realizing it's not Tatum's fault.

"You don't have to do this with me, Tate, but I can't be here, with them, around all the lies."

She sighs. "Madi, I'm not leaving you. I know our friendship moved fast, but... I've never had any friends before, and I'm a little..." Her face turns red before she looks back to me. "Lonely. So I'm not leaving you out here—alone."

"But you do realize that you'll have to ditch your credit cards?" I point out, watching her reaction.

Realization slips over briefly before a smile snaps back onto her face. "Yes, Madi. Consider them gone."

"Really?" I ask, my eyebrow quirked.

"Yes." She nods, and I almost buy it. Then she casually adds, "Right after I withdraw a few thousand."

Laughing, I shake my head, turning the music back up. What the fuck are we going to do?

"Okay," Tatum inserts, running her hand through her hair as she continues to drive us wherever the fuck we are going. "So we need to go back to your house quickly and gather whatever we might need."

"Like what?" I ask, horrified that we need to go back home. "No, Tate, I don't want to go there."

She looks to me. "Well, what then, Madi? We don't have many options, and we need passports and all that!"

"Okay," I whisper, resting into my seat and trying to think of a solution. "Okay, this is just a real blind shot, but I promise if this fails, we can break into my house and take whatever I need."

Tatum relaxes. "So where are we going?"

I swallow. "To Riverside. To the library."

Pulling up to the school, Tatum parks the car out front and turns in her seat to face me. "Are you sure about this?"

"Um." I search for the word I'm looking for, but fail. "No." I push open the door and get out just as Tatum's door closes.

"Well, lucky I have my running shoes on." She rounds the car and comes to stand next to me.

I look down at her feet. "Those aren't running shoes, Tatum."

Heading toward the school with Tatum in tow, we sneak down the side of the girls' classrooms, ducking under any windows where people might see us, and make our way past the pool, straight toward the library that's tucked behind the gym. As we reach the student-only entrance, I slide my student card over the little box until the green light flashes and beeps. Pulling open the door, we step inside. It's fairly quiet, a few students hanging about here and there, but no one who would take notice of Tatum and me. The door slips shut, breaking the kind of silence that can only come from a library.

Miss Winters's head snaps up to the entrance, pulling her out of the book she was engrossed in. Her eyes widen when she sees me, so I give her a pleading look. She gets to her feet, shoving her glasses up her nose. Walking toward Tatum and me, she watches her surroundings closely, her paranoia obvious.

"Girls, how can I help you?" She plasters on a fake smile.

"I know" is all I manage to say. All the times I've wanted to ask, *What the fuck is going on?* is replaced now with those two simple words.

Miss Winters pauses, her head tilting to the side as her eyes drift over my shoulder briefly before coming back to me. "You know?"

I maintain eye contact, my shoulders squaring. "I. Know." In a blink of an eye, she forcefully grabs onto Tatum's and my arms and directs us back toward the entrance we just walked through. Pushing the doors open, she shoves us back into the late afternoon sun, closing the doors behind herself.

She exhales, her hand coming up to her forehead where she rubs across it softly, in an almost meditating gesture. "Shit." She cranes her neck, closes her eyes, and then breathes out, "You know you're the Silver Swan?"

"The Silver what now?" Tatum asks sassily, looking toward me with a crinkled eyebrow.

"Yes," I hiss. "But I don't know what the fuck that means or how you know about it or why everyone has been lying to me."

"I can't...." Miss Winters shakes her head. "I'm sorry, Madison, but I can't get involved with all of it. It's too dangerous."

"Well then, can you help me disappear?"

Miss Winters snaps her head toward me. "You can't run from the Kings, Madison. They'll kill you." She ends her sentence in a whisper.

"They'll kill me anyway. Assuming I read the book correctly."

"Where is that book?" Miss Winters asks, looking around nervously.

"It's in my bag. Are you going to help me or not?"

She pauses, searches my eyes, and then pulls out her

phone. "Look, I know a guy. Tell him Tinker sent you."

"Tinker?" I ask as she scrolls through her cell.

She looks up at me. "Yes, Tinker." She pauses, dropping her arms to her side.

"What?"

"It's just…. Listen, you need to do this right if you're going to do it. Get all the documents he needs from you, but withdrawal all the cash you need for now. He's not cheap. You can't carry over ten grand in cash if you fly internationally, so withdrawal ten thousand, and then another eight to get everything you need from Benny." She pauses, giving me his number, and I quickly add it to my phone. "He will charge you four thousand each." She pauses and looks at me. "Run, Madi. Run and don't ever come back, because regardless of what Bishop feels about you?" She searches my eyes. "It means nothing. It meant nothing when it came to Khales, either."

"What do you mean? What do you know about Khales?"

Her face turns hard. "I know he put a bullet right between her eyes."

CHAPTER 2

After running back to Tatum's car, we both slip inside before she skids out and takes us toward the bank. "What the fuck does she mean? Bishop killed someone?" Tatum's eyes are wide as she looks between me and the road ahead.

"I don't think that was the first person he ever killed either," I murmur, looking outside my window.

"You never did tell me what you saw in that basement, Madi."

I want to tell her, but a strange part of me doesn't want her to know something that could be used against Bishop. *Stupid girl*, I scold myself. Also, it's safer for Tatum to not know anything.

"I don't really want to talk about it, Tate."

She smiles and pats my hand. "We're getting the fuck out

of here." Pulling up to the curb, we both jump out.

I close my door. "You go to your bank and I'll go to mine. We can carry ten each. That should get us through."

Tatum nods, but something flashes through her eyes and I pause. "Are you okay?"

"We're really doing this?" she quickly asks.

"You can back out now. I don't want to drag you into my mess anyway."

"No." She shakes her head. "I'm coming with you. I have nothing here."

I smile sadly. "Okay, then it's settled. Meet back here in ten minutes." Tatum nods and then quickly dashes into her bank as I cross the busy road to mine. Pushing open the doors with my head ducked, I collide into someone. "Sorry," I mutter, stepping around them.

"Madison?"

I look up to see Ridge staring back at me. "Oh, hi," I murmur, eyeing over his shoulder. I don't want to take long here; I need to get in and out as fast as possible, no stopping.

"Hey, I was going to come look for you. Have you heard from Tillie?" he asks, tilting his head. I look at him, properly this time, and notice the tired bags under his red-rimmed eyes and his disheveled hair.

"No, not since we came back from the cabin. Why? Is everything okay?" Now that he said that, it is odd I haven't noticed Tillie not contacting me. I've been so caught up in my shit that I haven't stopped to think.

He shakes his head. "No, no one has heard from her."

"I'll call her. I'm sure she's fine." She could be anywhere, but then again, she could really be okay. From what she told me about her dad, I'm not entirely surprised she hasn't gone home.

"Okay." He pulls out his phone. "Can I give you my number so you can call me if you hear from her? Please, I just want to make sure she's okay."

I nod, surveying inside toward the bank teller. I really need to leave. "Sure." He tells me his number, and I push it into my phone.... My phone! Shit! "Actually," I start, going for relaxed tone, "could you write it down?" He looks at me, pauses, but then nods, drawing out a pen and taking my hand, scribbling it down.

"Thanks, I'll call you." I sidestep away from him and walk the rest of the way into the bank. There's a fucking line. Of course there's a fucking line.

Fifteen minutes later, I'm walking out of the bank, tossing my ATM card into a trash can nearby, and heading back to the car.

Pulling open the passenger door, Tatum is smiling at me from the driver seat. "I actually feel really fucking excited about this."

"Makes one of us," I mutter, taking out my phone. "Drive." I pop open the glove compartment and pull out a pen and paper, transferring Ridge's number then scrubbing it off my hand. "I'll call Benny now."

Tatum nods as she continues to drive.

The phone rings until a deep voice picks up. "Who sent you?"

"Uh... uh...." I look around, confused. What a weird way to answer the phone. "Tinker?" God, I feel ridiculous saying that name out loud.

A pause.

Silence.

"The corner, on the last stretch of Highway 4."

8

"Uh, okay?"

He hangs up. I look down at my phone and then at Tatum.

"What'd he say?" she asks, looking between me and the road.

"We have to go to the corner on the last stretch of Highway 4."

Tate nods. "I know where that is."

"Give me your phone." I put my hand out to her. "Do you need any numbers from it?"

She pauses, eyes glassing over slightly before she squares her shoulders. "No. No one will even know I'm gone."

I smile sadly at her before winding my window down, tossing the cell out. Searching through my contacts, I take down a couple of numbers that might come in handy. Through my scrolling, my finger pauses over Bishop's name, and my heart sinks slightly.

Fuck him.

Not only did he kill Ally, but apparently he killed Khales too. I pass his name and keep searching until I get to my dad. My heart sinks further, but I keep scrolling up.

Nate.

I close my eyes, squeezing my phone in… frustration? Sadness? A combination of both? Winding down my window with my eyes still closed, I toss it out. "I don't need anyone either."

Pulling up to the almost abandoned crossroad off the highway, I notice it's empty—and it's getting late, the afternoon sun casting shadows through the large branches of trees that reside on the edge of the cul-de-sac.

"No one's here. It's quiet."

"Too quiet," I add. We pull to a stop and I get out of the car, slamming my door.

Tatum winds my window down. "Madi! Fuck's sake, can you not be a badass today, please? I don't want to die right now. Or ever."

I roll my eyes. "Miss Winters gave us this dude's number. She wouldn't fuck us over."

"You put an awful lot of confidence in Miss Winters," a voice says, a figure walking toward me out of the shadows. I spin around and see an older man making his way to me. He's wearing a hoodie and ripped dark jeans, and he must be in his midforties.

"Well, it's all I've got."

He nods in understanding. At first glance, no warning bells go off. "I've been in touch with Tinker. I have all your documents ready to go."

"That was quick."

"We have them at my beck and call. It's why I charge so much."

I shrug, not needing the details. "Let me see." He hands me two manila folders. One says Amira and the other says Atalia. Both last names. "We're sisters?" I look up at Benny. "Amira and Atalia Maddox? Could you not go with something simple?"

Benny looks at me deadpan. "Hand the money over."

I pull out the thick envelope and pass it to him. He takes out the cash and flicks through it. "I take it it's all here?"

"Of course. You know we're good for it."

He pauses, watching us for a split second before appearing satisfied with my answer. "This didn't happen.

Have a nice life, Amira."

I'm Amira? Of course I am. Stupid fancy name, it doesn't suit me at all.

I walk back to the car, swinging the door open, and hand Tatum the folder that says her new name on it. "Here you go, Atalia."

She scoffs, and then her smile drops. "Seriously?"

"Seriously."

"Well damn. Let's get this started." She puts the car in first gear and we drive to the closest airport.

Not long after, we're parking the car in the garage. We both get out and walk toward the building, me with my duffle bag and her with her own small bag.

"Where are we going?" Tatum asks, looking at me.

I squint my eyes at all the flights. Smiling, I nudge her with my elbow. "How long does it take to get a visa?"

CHAPTER 3

THE VISAS WERE RATHER EASY TO OBTAIN. THERE'S A kiosk counter set up toward the back of the airport, and since the country we're flying to has a direct agreement with the United States, all it took was a quick questionnaire online and done; we were accepted directly through the visa waiver system.

"I can't believe this," Tatum whispers. "We're going to New Zealand? Couldn't you choose a different country, like, I don't know... Dubai?"

I turn to face her. "And where do you think they'll look first, Tate?"

She sighs. "I guess so."

"And besides," I add, "I haven't even heard of New Zealand. I doubt Bishop has. And also..." I look toward her ungrateful ass, "it was either this or some small town in

Indonesia or Thailand."

"Could have got cheap new tits in Thailand."

Rolling my eyes, the voice overhead calls our flight name, and I look to Tatum, my heart beating in my chest. "Are you ready?"

She looks back at me and takes my hand. "Yeah… yeah, I am."

Two Months Later

"I don't know, Ta—Atalia."

Tatum grins at me, walking around the back of the bar in her skimpy shorts and lace push-up bra that hangs out of her ripped crop top. "Well, you know you can work here." She nods toward the stripper pole. We've been here for a couple of months now, and plan to stay for a couple more hopefully, but I need to find a job to keep my mind busy.

I turn back around and grin. "You know, I may not care anymore, but I won't be sucking on any poles." I take a sip of my drink and lean back in my chair, scanning the paper in front of me and flinging my pencil through my fingers. It's 12:00 p.m. here, which means it's around 8:00 p.m. the previous day back home.

Since coming here, Tatum and I have been staying in a little apartment right on the beach. We landed in Auckland thirteen hours after we boarded the plane and immediately purchased a little booklet of the country. We both agreed we wanted to be near the beach, grasping something that resembles home and keeping it close to us. So we found this small town in the middle of the north island called Mount

Maunganui. I can't pronounce it and have noticed a lot of the locals just call it The Mount.

It's beautiful here. Sandy beaches, big waves, little shops lining the main beach where houses and coastal homes are set up opposite. The entire strip of the shoreline goes on for around ten minutes by car and eventually takes you to another small suburb called Papamoa. New Zealanders are friendly—sometimes a little too friendly—the food is fresh, and the air is like walking into a sauna for the first time. It's lovely. But I haven't been able to find a job since we got here. The flat we live in is a small studio apartment—nothing over the top—but it costs a fortune. It turns out this town isn't exactly cheap to live in. Of course, trust Tatum and me to choose one of the more expensive towns in the whole of New Zealand. She found a job right away, working for cash in hand as a bartender-slash-stripper—I shit you not. I love Tatum, but I can see her slowly losing herself.

Is it happening to me too?

Whenever I try to dig inside, in search of my true feelings, I come up blank. I have none. I've thought once or twice about taking Tatum up on her offer and joining her as a stripper, but then I remembered I can't dance for shit and my ass jiggles a little more than it should.

"Nice drawing," the guy next to me interrupts my thoughts, pointing down to my piece of paper.

"Thanks," I murmur, leaning forward and taking my drink.

"How long did it take for you to draw that?"

"Hmmm." I swallow some of my drink and then look back at him. "About twenty minutes."

His eyebrows pull together. "Can I take a look?"

I nod. "Yeah, sure." I hand it to him, watching his expressions change. He has messy but well-styled light-brown hair, a five o'clock shadow, a straight pointy nose, and olive skin. His shoulders are square, much like his jaw, and he's wearing a dark leather jacket with a plain white shirt underneath, dark jeans, leather bangles on his wrists, and heavy black biker boots. Oh, God, please don't be a biker.

"These are fucking mint." He grins, studying my latest drawing. I don't know what the term "mint" means, but I take it it's some kind of New Zealand lingo. The drawing is a pink lotus flower that's half blossomed. There's a bullet sitting in the middle, the petals of the flower guarding it protectively. The shading isn't quite finished, but yeah, it's not bad.

"Thank you," I reply shyly.

He looks up at me. "I heard you tell your—" He looks toward Tatum on the pole. "—friend you're looking for a job?"

"Yeah." I nod. "We're from America."

"Backpacking?"

"Something like that," I answer through a tight smile.

"Jesse." He puts his heavily tattooed hand out.

I take it, surprised his palm is a little soft considering what he looks like. "Amira."

"Amira?" He grins. "Sort of sexy."

"Ha!" I laugh nervously. "Good one." Is he flirting? I can't tell.

His grin relaxes to a sly smirk. "Here." He slides his card across the bar. "I own Inked, the tattoo parlor two shops down." He points to my drawing. "I got you a job if you want it."

"What?" I gasp in disbelief. "I haven't tattooed anyone—ever!"

He shakes his head. "No, but I have, and do, and you draw fucking amazing. I can teach you. Or, you can just draw for me. I only do custom designs. So if you come in and sit down as I go over each client, you can draw what they say. Catch my drift?"

I swallow. "Shit."

"Scared?" He grins at me again, a dark eyebrow quirked.

"Sort of."

"Hey!" Tatum comes bouncing with bills stuffed under her bra. Jesus fucking Christ, this girl. She looks to Jesse and smiles, her eyes lighting up like the Fourth of July. She puts her hand out. "I'm Atalia!"

Jesse looks between us. "Similar names, or…?"

"Sisters," Tatum chirps, gripping onto the bar, jumping up, and planting her ass on top. Jesse walks over to her, picks her up from under her arms, and shakes his head.

"Don't go sitting your little ass on tabletops in this country, girl."

I laugh at Tate's pouted lip.

"Okay," I say to Jesse, and his eyes come directly back to me. "I mean," I correct, "I don't know if I'm what you're really looking for, but I'm willing to give it a try. Since, you know… I was rather close to going up"—I point toward the stage—"there."

He grins. "Yeah, come now." He nudges his head toward the front door, and I look between it and him and then back again.

"You're not a murderer, are you?"

"Guess you won't know until you follow me."

Pausing, my eyes lock onto his before I down my drink and get off the stool.

Turning to Tatum, I smile. "I'll be back soon."

She shrugs and then bounces back onto the stage. I follow Jesse out the door, the cool summer air hitting me across the face. He nudges his head toward the sidewalk.

"This isn't the part where you kill me, is it?" I chuckle, shoving my hands into my jean pockets.

He laughs, throwing his head back. "This is New Zealand, babe. You're safe." From what I've seen so far, it is safe here.

We walk down the sidewalk until we come to a shop that has black paint licked over the front with red stripes going diagonally down the brick structure. Jesse pulls out his keys, unlocks the door, and then ushers me inside.

Flicking the lights on, he gestures out in front of himself.

"It's clean!" is the first thing that comes into my brain, and me being me, of course I say it out loud.

Jesse laughs, closing the door behind himself to shut out the line of boy racers that are flooring it down the main street. "Yeah, I guess it sort of has to be." He tilts his head and then walks forward to the dark concrete counter. It's all rustic with a dose of modern. The floors are glass mirror tiles, and the seats are black leather with intricate designs carved into the armrests. All the booths are wide open but have the option to pull a curtain across for privacy. There's also a private booth at the back.

"Piercings and such," Jesse mutters, handing me a beer when he sees me looking at the booth.

"Thanks." I take it. "So what exactly do you want from me?"

He takes a swig and then looks at me. "When clients come in, you can sit in during their consultation, get a vision of what they want, and draw it for them. Just roughly sketch it."

"Okay, and when you don't have clients?" I ask, watching him carefully. He has a couple of beauty marks on his face that instantly draw my attention, so I look away quickly, not wanting to get caught ogling. He's a little more than hot. He has a rough sexiness about him. I wonder how old he is.

"You can stay at the front desk? I can pay you hourly plus give you a percentage out of the drawings you do—all cash in hand."

I think over his question and then look toward some of the artwork that's hanging on the walls. "I guess I'm in."

He steps forward, pushing his hands into the front pockets of his jeans, and tilts his head. "What's your story?"

Casually sucking in a breath, I bring the bottle to my mouth and swallow. "I don't really have one."

"Okay, and how long are you in NZ for?"

"Only for a couple of months. If that. So please don't think this is a permanent thing for me. I'd hate to give you the wrong impression."

The corner of his mouth tilts up slightly. "I'm not really into permanent."

I run my eyes up and down his body, once again failing to hide my attraction to him, but anytime I think, *Okay, I can do this. I can find a man just to have something casual with,* Bishop possesses my body and my thoughts. It's not entirely fair, considering he has probably moved on already, but it's just not in me to do it yet. It's too soon.

I halt him with my hand, sensing he was going to go into the dating territory. "Please don't. Not yet."

He grins. "I can do not yet."

Handing him my barely touched beer, I smile at him. "I better go, but I'll see you tomorrow?"

"Yup, 9:00 a.m.," he agrees.

I nod, turn on my heel, and walk out the door. Figuring I'll walk the rest of the way back to our apartment instead of calling a taxi, I eventually make my way to the main beach. Stepping down the sandy steps, I inhale the thick, salty ocean air and close my eyes, shutting out any noise but the crashing of waves and the crickets chirping within the trees. New Zealand is beautiful; there's no doubt about that. But I miss being home in the US. I don't know what's happening back home. No one has found me, or no one has looked—not sure which of the two is correct.

"You okay?" Tatum comes down the steps and walks to where I'm standing. I take a seat on the sand and draw my knees up, my hair falling over my shoulders.

"Not really."

Tate plops down beside me, her long coat wrapped tightly around her body.

"Are you wearing clothes under that?"

"What?" She bats her eyelashes innocently. "Of course I am! And also…." She pulls out a bottle of whiskey and what I'm pretty sure is a joint. "Tada!"

I shake my head and laugh. "You're a hot mess, you know that?"

"I know," she sighs, resting her head on my shoulder. "Be a hot mess with me?"

I swallow, looking out to the dark ocean, wondering what lies are on the other side of what seems to be an endless bank of water. "Yeah, I think I'm ready to be just that."

The thoughts of Bishop and my dad have been eating

away at me ever since I left the US. Maybe the reason why it's not affecting Tatum so much is because she's always high or drunk—or having sex. Although I'm not ready for the sex part—and I don't even know why, because it's not like Bishop and I were together—I still feel like I'm betraying him. Why the fuck should I care if I'm betraying him though? He betrayed me! He lied, cheated, manipulated, and killed someone. He's exactly—

"Make it stop, Tate," I whisper through fresh tears as my throat clogs. A single tear trickles over my cheek and Tatum catches it with her index finger. She then grips my chin, turning me to face her. She searches my eyes, and for a second, she seems stone-cold sober. "We will make it stop together, Mads."

Swallowing, I nod and take the joint from her. Lighting it up, I put it between my lips and inhale deeply until my lungs catch on fire and my throat turns to stone. Blowing out the smoke, a sputter of coughs come out of me, so I snatch the whiskey from her hand while passing her the joint. After twisting the cap, I bang on my chest and then put the tip to my lips and swallow, allowing the burning of the cheap whiskey to coat my already parched throat.

Tatum falls onto her back with the joint tucked between her lips and I lay back with her, the stars swimming in the dark abyss of the sphere, a bottle of whiskey between my fingers, and my hair sprawled out over the sand.

"Do you think he ever cared, Tate?" I whisper, tilting my head and lining up the southern cross that hangs brightly in the sky.

"Bishop? No. Nate? Yes." She coughs loudly, banging on her chest. I sit up, taking a drink until the burning turns my throat numb and my head throbs with intoxication. Tatum passes me the joint. "Sorry, Mads. I just don't think he did. But I wouldn't take it personally. He doesn't give a fuck about anyone or anything." I toke on the ganja, this time holding it in longer to intensify my buzz, and then blow it out slowly.

"Why the fuck can't I bring myself to get laid."

"That will come, babe. I said he didn't care. I'm well aware that you did."

"I'm stupid."

"No." Tatum shakes her head, handing me the whiskey. "No, you're not. You're Madison Montgomery, and you're a fucking boss-ass bitch who feels, Mads. That's a big deal. More people should feel."

"Felt," I whisper, my tears now dry. "They used me as their puppet. Now I'm broken."

"Broken but hot, and who, by the way, has found a hot tattoo artist!"

I laugh, pulling my bottom lip into my mouth. "He is a bit hot, huh?"

"A bit?" Tatum looks offended. "Honey, he will do you fine until our next stop."

"Have you decided where we're going next?" I slur, my eyes narrowing on her to try to focus.

"Mmmm, Milan?"

"Spain?" I ask, shocked. "What about London? Can we do Bristol?"

"Why?"

"I don't know. Just really want to find a hot British guy."

"To bang, or to complain to me about how you can't bang?"

I laugh, shoving her shoulder. "Shut up. Come on." I get

up off the sand and pull Tatum with me. Only we both spin out and… I'm falling. I land on the sand with a plonk, the hard surface sure to bruise my ass.

"Fuck!" Tatum curses behind a chuckle.

I can't help it. Undiluted laughter erupts out of me, and I clutch my belly. "Holy shit." I shake my head, my cheeks now aching from all the smiling.

"Well that's a laugh I haven't heard in a while." Tatum clutches her stomach, wiping the tears from her eyes.

"Yeah, I promise I'll try to do it more."

CHAPTER 4

"Morning, hot stuff." Tatum walks into my room, a joint between her fingers.

"Morning," I answer, pulling on some cutoff shorts and a tight tank. "Is this too much?"

"Nonsense!" Tatum hushes my insecurities, stepping forward and handing me the joint. She pushes my tits up and ruffles my hair. "This is a tattoo parlor!"

I bring the smoke to my lips and take a hit. "True!" I agree, before handing it back to her and walking out to the living room. Our apartment—or flat, as they call it here—is small. It has two bedrooms, a small living room, and a kitchenette that overlooks the main beach strip. We pay a small fortune to live here too, but it's what Tatum wanted, and since she was the only one working at the time, I let her do it. Our savings are still healthy, thanks to Tatum working pretty much right away, but that's the money we have to live on when we skip countries. The kitchenette is a mustard yellow, and the living room is neutral beige. It's a beach house, and the family we rent it from also own the bar Tatum works at. It worked in our favor, and we were really lucky.

After pouring my coffee, I bring it to my lips. "Work tonight?"

Tatum nods. "Yep. What time do you finish?"

I shake my head. "I don't know. We didn't really talk about that."

"Jesse?" Tatum asks. "He's interesting-looking, right? What's the NZ nationality?"

"I don't know, and I'm not asking."

"He looks Cuban or something."

"You finished?" I ask as she gazes off into the sky, resting her feet on the wooden coffee table. The flat came furnished with just the necessities. Sofas, fridge, beds. There's no television, but we don't really need it.

"Okay, see you after work." I wave to Tatum, who is still smoking her joint. Figuring it's probably a ten-minute stroll down to the main town strip, I decide to walk instead of catching the bus. Saving money and all that too. I get there five minutes later, and sucking in a deep breath, I push open the doors and step inside. Some rock song is playing that I haven't heard before, but I kinda dig it, and I step toward the front desk where a girl with pitch-black hair and a whole lot of ink is sitting.

"Hi," I say to her.

She looks up at me from the computer. "Hey! What can I help you with?"

"This one's mine," Jesse announces, stepping out from

24

behind one of the closed booths. I know he didn't mean it as in *I'm his*, but I squirm anyway. I hate that I squirm. I'm an idiot for squirming. Yet I want to swoon.

"New girl?" the dark-haired girl asks Jesse.

Jesse nods. "Yeah, this is Amira. She's the artist I told you about last night."

"Oh, right!" she says, clicking her fingers in recognition. "Hi! I'm Kiriana!"

"Ki-what-what?" I ask, shocked, my eyes fluttering. "Sorry, I'm… can you break it down for me?"

Kiri something laughs and pats the seat beside her. "Kiri, like kitty only you roll the R, and -ana, which is… yeah, -ana!"

"Kiriana?" I say, sounding ridiculous because my accent just won't let me roll anything, so I end up pronouncing it like ki-ree-ana.

She waves me off. "That'll do. Come, sit. Show me what you got."

Jesse winks at me and then walks back to his booth. After drawing for two different clients, I get off at 5:00 p.m. Picking up my bag, I nudge my head at Jesse. "Thanks for today. I needed it."

"No problem." He winks again. I smile and then walk out the door, heading straight to the bar Tatum works at.

Pushing open the doors, it's pretty empty because of the time. A few people are scattered around the place, but it's nothing like when it's in full swing.

"Hey!" Tatum smiles, waving me over to the bar. I grin and start walking toward her. I need to get Bishop out of my head one way or another so I might take the way that has an endless supply of alcohol. Taking a seat, Tatum pours a shot and slides it over to me. "Bottoms up, bitch!" I clink her glass and then toss it back.

"Yeah." I smirk. "Bottoms up," I say and slam the shot glass down onto the bar. The Weeknd's "Or Nah" starts pulsating through the room and I bang on the bar. "Another!"

"That's the spirit," Tatum squeals, pouring me another shot. She twirls the bottle between her fingers like a pro, and I narrow my eyes, knocking my shot back. "How'd you learn to do that, *Coyote Ugly*?"

"What? Not bad, huh?" She does it again and I roll my eyes.

"Show off," I tease, throwing back another shot.

Hours and many shots later, I get up off the bar stool, my head spinning. "Wooo." I reach for the edge of my stool, looking around the now fully decked-out club.

I lean over the bar and into Tatum. "I need to pee. Be right back!"

She nods, shooing me off. Dead Prez's "Hip Hop" starts playing, and I push through the crowd, making a beeline for the toilet. Walking into one of the stalls, I shove my pants down and let it all go. Sighing, I reach for my burner phone and pull it out of my pocket as it rings. Who even knows this number?

"Hello?" I slur, smiling at how drunk I am.

"You think you can fucking run from me, kitty? Nah-uh."

I scream and drop the cell, quickly standing from the toilet and shoving my pants back on. Reaching for my phone, I toss it into the toilet bowl, flushing it furiously, and then run out of the stall, my heart beating in my chest. Holy fuck! How did Bishop get my number?

That voice.

Pushing back through the crowd, I look directly at Tatum until I come face-to-face with her.

"We need to leave."

"What?" she asks over the deep bass.

"We. Need. To leave. Now!" I borderline scream at her, though it's slurred because of all the alcohol.

She searches my eyes until understanding sets in. "Oh, fuck."

"Yes, fuck is right."

She nods, tugging off her apron and throwing it on the bar. Running around to me, she snatches a bottle, and we hurry out of the bar.

Jesse.

Shit. I don't even have time to tell him I won't be coming back. Maybe I could leave a note under the parlor door. No, I can't risk it.

We catch a taxi to the flat, and as soon as we get inside, we start pulling out our bags. I rush into the bathroom, scooping up all my toiletries, and then walk into the closet, pulling down the little safe I keep my money in, throwing it into my bag. After I'm sure all my shit is gathered, I go out to meet Tatum.

"Ready?" I ask.

She nods, wheeling her suitcase. "Yes, yup, shit."

I glance down at my suitcase and then back to Tatum. "It was Bishop. How did he find my number?"

"Mads, I've already told you. "They own the school and their level of pull that they have on people is mysterious, to say the least."

"I guess they still want to kill me."

"Kill you?" she asks, shocked.

Shaking my head, I wipe my frown with a smile, nudging my head toward the door. "I guess it's time for Bristol."

CHAPTER 5

THE GLASS SLIDING DOORS OPEN OUT ONTO A chillier atmosphere than what was in New Zealand. It's almost December, so I guess we chose a cooler time to come to this side of the country, as opposed to New Zealand, where it's summer in December. Not that we had a choice or anything. Tatum comes up beside me, her teeth jittering. "Jesus, let's choose a warmer place next time."

I smile at her, waving down the taxi that's pulling up beside the curb. It stops in front and I run to the passenger window. "Are you free?"

He nods. "Yep!" Then he pops the trunk for both of us to put our bags into.

"Where are we staying, exactly?" Tatum whispers.

I shrug, putting my bags into the trunk. "I don't know. I guess we'll ask him to take us to a cheap motel or whatever it is they call it here."

"Good idea." Tatum nods, getting into the back seat.

A few days later, after finding a good little place to stay in, "Hail to the King" by Avenged Sevenfold is pumping through the massive speakers, shaking the floor. I tip my drink back and Tatum winks at me.

"I think I'm going to like it here." She looks around until her eyes land on two guys who are so obviously checking us out.

"Come." She grins, gripping onto my hand.

"Tate—"

"Mads, please, when are you going to get over this shit with Bishop? He's a liar and doesn't deserve you!" Her hands come up to my cheeks. "Repeat after me."

I suck my bottom lip into my mouth to stifle my laugh.

"Bishop Vincent Hayes is a cocksucker," she says calmly, waiting for me to repeat.

A giggle erupts out of me from all the alcohol. "Bishop Vincent Hayes is a cocksucker."

"Atta girl, now..." She tips her head back, swallowing her shot in one go. "Speaking of sucking cock." Then she pulls me through the crowd of people until we're in front of the two guys who were eye fucking us.

"Hi, boys." Tatum grins. "Which one of you is buying us a drink?"

They both launch off their chairs. "Subtle," I snicker under my breath.

Not my type at all.

The ground starts swimming, or it's swimming in my mind when one of the guys pulls me into him.

"Wanna dance, pretty girl?"

Pretty girl? I shrug, because what can a dance do? He pulls me onto the floor just as "Bad Things" by Machine Gun Kelly starts playing. It's more of an understated beat and a little personal, but whatever. It's not like we're at a nightclub or anything; this place is just a bar. It's actually under the room we're staying in, and we thought we'd check it out. Homeboy pulls me into his chest again—a chest that is the complete opposite of Bishop's. A little squishier than I'd like, and when I look down, I see his beer belly.

Oh gross. Nope, I can't do this.

"Sorry," I push at his chest, "I can't do this."

"Nonsense." He grins, saliva covering his mouth.

"Yeah," I answer again, pushing at his chest. "Just not really feeling it." He grips my wrist and pulls me into him again. "Hey!" I yell, though it's still a slur. Where's Tatum? I spin around, trying to find her, but I can't see her anywhere. He starts to drag me toward a back door that has an exit light flashing over the top.

"No." I try to pull my hand out of his grip, only it doesn't move. He tugs me roughly, and I look around to see if anyone knows what he's doing, but the music is too loud, and there are too many people to know what's happening. Reaching the door, he pushes it open and my eyes shut, consciousness coming in and out. Oh no.

"Stop," Tatum moans in the distance.

"Tatum!" I look down the dark alley and see the other guy with her, tugging her dress up.

"Little American slags," the guy who is pulling me mutters. "We'll show you."

"No!" I scream, shoving at his chest. Oh my God, why

do my limbs feel like Jell-O, and why am I in heat? I rub my thighs together in an attempt to calm the throbbing need that has started, but nothing happens. If anything, the feeling intensifies. I launch toward the fat shit, scratching him across his face until I can feel his flesh peel away and clog under my fingernails.

"You bitch!" He slams me up against the brick wall, my head smashing against it with a crack.

"Tatum, wake up. Stay with me." The guy who has her has pulled off her panties. The guy who has me up against the wall starts to make a beeline for my own. "Get the fuck off me, you fat slob!" I won't cry. No way in fucking hell will I cry. I look at him square in the eye. "If you so much as come near me with that stubby thing you call a cock, I will rip it off."

He laughs. "I doubt that, honey." Then he tears off my panties, clutches me around my upper thighs roughly until his fingertips are digging into my flesh, and hikes me up the wall. "Open up like the good little snatch you are."

I roll my tongue and spit in his face, just as a gun blasts off in the distance, blood and brain matter spraying all over my face. His eyes pop in shock for a split second before he drops to the ground in a shallow thud. A blood-curdling scream ripples out of me, and then Tatum screams as another pop sounds off and the guy who is clutching her falls to the ground, the flesh on his scalp turning to dust, spraying all over Tatum.

She screams, and I drop to the ground, blackness coming in and out. Just as hands scoop under me, I hear a "Fucking stupid bitch" before sleep takes hold.

CHAPTER 6

SOMETHING JOLTING UNDERNEATH MY BODY WAKES ME. Looking to the side, confused about where I am, memories start to take hold. I gasp, sucking in a breath. There, sitting on the seat beside me, is Bishop.

Fuck.

"Surprised?" he asks, his eyebrow quirked.

I clear my throat. "Well, no, actually."

He clenches his jaw, so obviously frustrated. "That's it." He shakes his head, whispering under his breath, "I'm locking you in the basement until this shit is sorted."

"What?" I shriek, and that's when the sting and the taste of metal touch the tip of my tongue. I touch my lip, memories flooding through my brain. "Oh, fuck!" I lean over, holding in my gag.

"Jesus, Kitty, out the fucking window!"

I hit the button blindly until the window cranks down. "You, you killed them."

"I did."

"You kill people?"

"I do."

"Why?" I yell, just as my stomach heaves again and I lean out the window, spilling all of whatever I last ate out into the dry night air. Leaning back in, wiping my mouth, I look back to him through blurry eyes. "Why, Bishop?"

"For reasons you will never understand, Madison." He looks toward Tatum, who is lying flat on the seat in front of us. I don't know whose limo we're in. Everything seems dreamlike.

"She's asleep. I didn't kill her." He interrupts my thoughts with a bored tone.

"Well, I appreciate it." I roll my eyes, failing at my attempt to not be snarky.

"Watch your fucking mouth, Madison. This is your fault. All of this!" His arms stretch wide. "You started a fucking war when you left that day."

"Me?" I burst out. "How the fuck is that possible?" The tangy aftertaste of my being sick simmers at the back of my throat. "You did this. All of you! I still don't understand anything!"

"How much of the book did you read?" he asks, leaning forward and bracing his arms over his knees.

"The book?" I question, tilting my head back on the headrest. My mind still swims in a daze.

"The book, Madison, the book!"

"Oh." I clear my throat. "Um, only quarter of the way through. Why?"

"Do you have it on you?"

"It's in my bag back at our place."

Bishop leans forward and taps on the glass that separates us from the front seat. The window cranks down. He orders the driver to take us back to our place, the exact address.

"Wow!" I shake my head, my hands going up.

Bishop leans back into his seat. "What?" he snaps.

"How'd you know where I live?"

He laughs, pulling his hoodie over his head. "It's cute you think I'd let you get out of this alive, Kitty, and I've always known where you lived. This little detour in the limo right now is just so you calm down enough to pack your shit."

Pulling up to our low-class flat and the bar, I get out of the car, slamming the door behind me, which wakes Tatum from her deep slumber.

"Wait!" Bishop gets out, shutting the door. Ignoring his intrusive behavior, I start walking toward the side stairs in the back alley. "Madison!" he yells, his heavy footsteps getting louder and louder. "Would you fucking wait?" He grips onto my arm, tugging me backward.

I let out a frustrated scream, yanking my arm out of his grip. "Can you fucking not? God! You—"

His hand flies up to my throat, leaving me gasping for air. Pushing me backward until my back slams against the bricks, he steps between my thighs and grazes me higher up the wall. "First of all," he squeezes until I'm sure my face is going to burst, "don't fucking forget who the fuck you're talking to." He tilts his head, glancing over my face. "Second of all, you don't get to throw your fucking weight around, Madison. I'll lock you in a cage as soon as we get you back to the Hamptons if you don't watch your fucking mouth." He releases me, my feet hitting the ground.

"Fuck you." Spinning around, I run up the metal stairs, push open the door, and head straight to my bedroom, fighting back the tears that are threatening to surface. Where the hell is my dad? Why is it that Bishop is the one who was sent to "collect" me? Did I really think I could run from them? Well yes, yes I did. Pulling open my closet, I start tearing my clothes off the hangers and throwing them onto my bed just as Bishop walks in.

"You have five minutes to get everything that means anything to you and get back downstairs. You try to run," Bishop says, his voice dipping, "and I'll kill you myself. I'm done playing games." Then he walks out and leaves me in my room, clutching the dark sequined dress I wore last weekend—back when things weren't so complicated. I mean, as complicated as us being on the run from my psychopathic whatever he is. Ex? No. That doesn't sound right.

"Jesus," Tatum murmurs, walking in, her hair all over her face. She rubs the palm of her hand over her forehead. "What the hell happened?"

"You passed out," I mutter, still annoyed at Bishop and shoving clothes into my suitcase. "And you have five minutes to pack before Bishop carries us both out."

"I saw that." Her eyes widen. "So he found us, huh?"

I chuckle, walking into the bathroom to grab my toothbrush. "No, we were never lost from him."

CHAPTER 7

L ANDING BACK IN THE HAMPTONS WASN'T AS BAD AS I thought it would be. Despite the fact that Bishop refused to even glance my way for the entire flight, I guess a sense of calm has come over me. Running is tiring. Keeping up with your aliases and fake appearances… I was tired of it to a degree. Did I want to get caught? No. But at the same time, it's like it's finally over.

Or just begun.

Stepping down off the steps and onto the tarmac, I grip onto Tatum's arm and tug her forward.

"Ouch!" she protests. "Geez, Mads, I'm fragile right now."

"What are we going to do, Tate?" I whisper as we head toward the awaiting black stretch limo. "I mean, seriously, what if they kill us?"

She rolls her eyes, pulling her arm out of my grip.

"Madison, they're not going to kill you. You're being dramatic." She looks at me and I narrow my eyes. "Fuck," she exhales. "Fine, okay. Well, if they do, I won't go down without a fight. All right?"

"Tatum." I shake my head.

"Move." Bishop shoves me toward the limo. I snarl at him, gripping the door handle just as a black Audi Q7 flies down the strip, skidding to a halt in a cloud of smoke. I wave the smoke away from my face and squint my eyes.

"Jesus fucking Christ," Bishop curses, shoving me behind himself.

"Nah-uh!" a voice barks behind the cloud.

I know that voice.

"Nate!" I yell, running toward the smoke and straight into his arms. He's wearing his trademark red baseball cap flipped backward. I've never been so fucking happy to see that stupid cap. Pulling me into his chest, he lifts me off the ground, and I wrap my legs around him.

"Hey, Kitty, how you been?" He squeezes me into him.

"Not good," I answer truthfully. I didn't realize just how much I missed Nate until I heard his voice. I don't know if it's fair that I forgive him and not Bishop, but at the same time, Nate hasn't threatened my life a hundred times within the space twenty-four hours.

Nate steps backward, his hands dropping down to mine. "It had to be done, sis. You know that." He searches my eyes. "Right?" I pull my bottom lip into my mouth. "Listen, things have changed. If Bishop didn't come get you, someone else would have, only you wouldn't be coming home in a seat on that plane. You'd be coming home in a box."

I exhale. "I just... I... I guess we have a lot to talk about."

"Yeah." Nate smiles, but it doesn't reach his eyes. "I guess we sort of do." He looks directly over my shoulder and grins. "Oh, come on." I throw a glance over my shoulder to see Bishop flipping Nate off. He tugs on my arm and points to his car. "Get in." Then he looks to Tatum. "You too!"

Tatum huffs and then stomps toward the car. Slipping my seat forward, I let her slide into the back before pushing it back into place and getting into the front. As I close the door, she whispers from behind me, "What do you think this is all about?"

"I don't know," I answer, watching Nate and Bishop talk. "I mean, I know some, but not a lot. At least not right now." I close my mouth, thinking about *the* book. They know I still have it. Will the boys let me read it? Are they still going to hide information from me?

Yes. I don't trust them at all. Though I'm probably dreaming, I've never gone down without a fight, so it's my turn to start playing the dealer, and these boys are about to become my pawns.

Nate pulls open the driver-side door and slides in. "So where are we going?"

I shrug, watching as Bishop gets into the limo and it slowly pulls away. "Take me somewhere."

Nate winks at me then puts the car in reverse until we're skidding out in a cloud of smoke. "I know just the place."

CHAPTER 8

"WHY CAN'T I COME?" TATUM MOANS, STOMPING HER FOOT JUST AS SHE GETS OUT OF NATE'S CAR.

NATE POINTS TOWARD HER FRONT DOOR. "GET YOUR ASS INSIDE, WOMAN! I'LL DEAL WITH YOU ON MONDAY. AT SCHOOL!"

I whip my head toward him just as Tatum trots off in defeat. "School?" I squeak. "No. No. No. No!" I shake my head, leaning into my door. "No, fuck no, Nate!"

"Hey!" He grins, putting the car into first gear and driving forward. "Not my orders, sis."

"Oh, okay!" I snap. "And whose orders are they? Because I swear to God, Nate, if you say Bishop, I will kill you. And don't play with me, because I've seen enough death to not flinch if I need to put a bullet between your pretty little eyes."

"I see you're still a badass."

"I see you're still not very smart!" I quip, shuffling in my seat to face forward. There's a long pause of awkward silence.

"Look, here's the thing. I get that you're all fucked up and broken and messed up in the head over all this shit that's going on, sis, but this goes a lot deeper than you could even wrap your mind around."

"Are you going to tell me what this is?" I ask, looking back at him.

He gives an instant "No."

"Then fuck you. We're done here." I lean forward and hit the radio until The Game's "It's Okay" fills the silence. What does he mean orders? What—Bishop? Or has something else happened since I've been gone? My dad hasn't reached out to me. Did he know Bishop would be after me? If what Bishop said is true, and if he really did know where I was all along, why did they never take the opportunity and get me? Nothing makes sense, as usual. Leaning my head on the cool window, I close my eyes and try to think of happier times.

"Madison! Don't touch that!" my mother scolded me, hitting my hand away from the pretty blue frosting.

"Why? I'm hungry!" I demanded, reaching for the cake again.

"Because it's not for you and you have to learn how to be patient."

"But whose cake is it?" I asked, tilting my head. I always thought my mom was beautiful. She had long brown hair and kind hazel eyes. Dad said I got his eyes because mine are green, but I think I have some of my mom's eyes too, because they twinkle in the sun.

"Madison." My mom smiled, looking over my shoulder.

"Honey." Her hands came to my shoulder. "I want you to meet someone."

"Okay, but who?" I wasn't really a small girl. I mean, I was turning five soon. That wasn't small anymore; that was old enough to start school.

"Madison!" Nate snaps me out of my haze. I turn to face him, swiping the tears off my cheeks.

"Yeah?"

"You okay?" he asks, looking between me and the road ahead of him.

"I'll be fine."

I won't be fine.

Pulling up to our house, I turn in my seat to face Nate. Gazing into his eyes, I smile. "You know... I don't like you boys much."

His hand comes over his chest in mock insult. "Really?" he gasps, his eyes wide. "Who would have known?"

"Shut up." I shove him. "You coming in?"

"I've just got to go handle something. I'll be home a little later."

"Letting me face the 'rents on my own, huh?" I ask, inspecting the modern-style brick house. The house I've come to call home.

"Sorry, sis, but hey!" he calls out, just as I get out of the car. "If you need like an alibi or anything, I'm your guy." I roll my eyes and slam the door behind me. If there's anyone I will need an alibi for, it'll be against him and his pack, not our parents. Exhaling, I step toward the house and push open the front door. The scent of disinfectant, flowers blossoming, and tarnished wood floats around the familiar surroundings.

"Hello?" I call out, shutting the door behind me and dropping my bag.

"Madison?" Elena calls out, stepping out of the kitchen and wiping her hands. "Oh my God!" She runs toward me and squeezes me into her chest. Tears wet the side of my neck and I inch back, slightly confused.

"Are you okay? Where have you been? What happened?" She panics, her hands running up and down my arms. "Jesus, Madison, your father and I have been worried sick!" Confusion wiggles itself under my skin. No one told her anything? Not even Nate?

"S-sorry," I mutter, unknowing what story I should be going with. Fucking Nate, couldn't even give me a heads up before I got out of the car.

"Sorry?" she squeals, her hands running over my cheeks. "I was worried, Madison. So was your father. Come on, let's get you something to eat." I follow her into the kitchen, tugging out one of the stools and taking a seat. She pulls open the fridge and takes out some deli meats.

"Do you want to talk about it?"

Shaking my head, I answer, "No. Sorry. Not right now. Where's Dad?"

Putting the sandwich together, she cuts it and then slides my plate toward me. "He'll be home soon. I'll call him to let him know you're home."

"Okay, thank you." Picking up the sandwich, I take a small bite and chew slowly. The dry bread and lettuce isn't helping my parched throat, so I slide off the stool and go to the fridge, taking out the carton of OJ. Closing the fridge, I see a note dangles on the door, but it's written in some foreign, weird-ass language. Latin, I think. I vaguely remember a friend talking about Latin back at one of my old schools, and the words look similar. Why would there be a note written in Latin on our fridge? It's a dead language; no one uses it anymore, which makes it even more absurd. It would make more sense if the note was written in Japanese.

Tugging it off the magnet, I read over the fancy wording.

Saltare cum morte solutio ligatorum inventae sunt in verbis conectuntur et sculptilia contrivisset in sanguine et medullis.

Pulling out my phone from my back pocket, I punch the wording into Google Translate.

Riddles dance with death when the words are inked in blood and carved with marrow.

The words hit me like a train of destruction. Why would this be on our fridge? Why today of all days? I flip the note over and scan the back. The paper is fresh, the ink clean. It doesn't look old at all, and—

"Madison, your father is on his way home." Elena walks in, and I quickly push the note into my back pocket.

"Okay." I smile.

She points to my sandwich. "Eat up."

After eating, I climb the stairs and head to my room. I push open my bedroom door and pause at the threshold. Everything is exactly as I left it. My four-poster bed is rooted in the same spot, my net curtains still shade my patio door, and my TV is still sitting nicely on my dresser at the foot of my bed. Walking into my closet, I pull off some hangers and toss them onto the bed. I know I need to unpack and get settled back into my life here, but I have a plan to carry out, and following through will take a lot of time and preparation.

Emptying my duffle bag into my clothes basket, I swipe my hair out of my face just as a thump hits the top of my laundry. Bending down, my fingers skim over the worn leather, curving over the emblem embossed into the cover. Tilting my head, I suck in my bottom lip and pick it up, flipping the pages as I make my way back to my bed. Whatever my plan is, I need to continue this book—or diary, or suicide note. It's the key to everything; I just know it.

Flicking through, I land on the chapter I was up to, after finding out about the Silver Swans.

9.
The Silver Swan

The truth is I don't know what my husband did to my daughter. He said girls are tainted. There's no room for girls in his master plan, and that's how it always will be. He said they would sell the girls, but something dark and doubtful always tickles the back of my mind. My husband is a liar, a cheat, and a manipulator. There's absolutely no part of him that is truthful or redeemable.

Later that night, after my maid had cleaned me up, Humphrey came back into the cave, sat down beside me, and said, "Girls cannot be born into our covenant, wife. They're weak by human nature. They must be taken care of at their birth."

"You're not God, Humphrey. You cannot deem who bears what when pregnant."

"No," he replied simply. "But I can take care of it."

I shook my head, my heart in tatters, and my life turning bleak, dark, finished. "There will be no Silver Swans born into this family or any of the first nine. They will be demolished."

"Silver Swans?" I asked, clipped and annoyed.

"The Silver Swan is, in old times, what they would call a tarnished being. Every girl born into the first nine is a tarnished being. It's no place for a her."

"Humphrey Haynes!" I exasperated, trying to calm my frantic beating heart. I leaned toward him, inching closer until my lips were a mere whisper away from his cheek. "Did you have our daughter killed?"

He brought his cold, dead eyes up to mine and grinned a devilish grin that churned my stomach. "I did. And every girl after her will also be taken care of. Girls have no place in our lineage."

I inched backward, my heart sinking in my chest and my eyes watering with grief. "I—I...," I whispered, speechless in the heartless way Humphrey spoke about our child. My heart snapped in two. "I have to leave." I ran out of the room and into the forest, the leaves and branches shielding me from the full moon. Kneeling down, I let my tears overflow and my grief overpower me. Crying, yearning for my daughter that I will never know.

I suck in a breath, slamming the book closed. He killed her? And all other Silver Swans? Why? Why am I still alive, and how am I still alive? Are there any more like me?

There's a knock on the door that pulls me out of my frantic thoughts.

"Come in." My door opens, and my dad stands in the threshold, his hands pushed into the pockets of his slacks.

"Thinking of running away again?" he asks, his head tilting.

"Are you going to be honest with me?" I retort.

He steps into the room and closes the door behind

himself. Dad still looks the same, young, fit, with a sprinkle of gray hair on the sides of his head. "Madison, I can't answer all the questions you're going to ask."

I inch up onto my knees. "What does that mean exactly? You, Dad, I trusted you."

"Madi," he whispers, shaking his head. "This world... it's complicated."

"I'm the Silver Swan?"

His eyebrows tug together in worry. "Yes." He takes a seat on my bed and looks toward *The Book*. "Have you read much more?"

I follow his eye line and nod. "A little bit. They kill the girls? So why am I still alive?"

He looks at me out of the corner of his eye. "Because I was supposed to keep you safe, Madison. Your mother and I, we love you very much."

"Mom's death," I whisper, "was it what I was told?"

Dad looks at me. "No. It's more complicated than what you know."

"What?" I screech, shooting off the bed. "Explain."

"Madison!" Dad's voice booms with an authoritative tone. "I will tell you what I think you need to know right now. Any other questions will have to wait. Do you understand?" His eyes narrow as he pushes up off my bed. He brushes my cheek. "I love you, Madison, but this is not something you can pry into. I need you to just leave it to me and the Kings." He leans down so his eyes are square with mine. "Do you understand what I'm saying?" I understand what he's saying, but there's no way I'm going to sit on my hands and be left guessing. Not like last time. But I nod, because that's not something Dad needs to know or worry about—right now.

"Yes. I understand." I swallow past the lump in my throat. He nods, a small smile spreading across his face. "Now get some rest so you're ready for school in the morning." He walks back toward my door and yanks it open. "Oh, and Madison?" he adds, looking at me over his shoulder. "Elena doesn't know anything. She thinks you ran off for a couple months to be rebellious. I'd like to keep it that way."

"Sure," I whisper. "Night, Dad." He leaves, shutting the door behind him. I walk into my closet and pull out some pajamas before slipping into my bathroom, flicking the lock on Nate's side. Stepping into the hot cascading water, I scrub the last two months off my skin.

CHAPTER 9

"So what did your dad say?" Tatum asks, sucking the juice of her orange off her fingertips. Being back in the atrium isn't as weird as I thought it would be. It's like Ally didn't exist, though. Like everyone just forgot that she had gone, or died, or whatever they thought. What did they know? I understand we'd been gone for a couple of months, but you would think a death in such a small school would impact it a lot longer than that.

"Uh, he didn't say much. Just gave me the rundown about how I need to keep things away from Nate's mom."

Tate pauses. "Why? Hey." She leans in closer, checking to make sure no one can hear her. "What the hell is going on? You know you can trust me, Mads."

I know I can; that's not my issue with Tatum, never has been. I trust her with my life, but it's the people you trust with your life who you want to protect the most. Telling Tatum every single thing about this… life would only put her in danger.

"I know, Tate," I whisper back to her. "You know that if I could, I would tell you everything, but I can't."

"Can't or won't?" she snaps at me.

"Won't!" I reply, leaning back into my seat. "Now ca—"

"Mads?"

I turn in my seat. "Carter? Hey!" I smile, standing.

He pulls me into his chest. "Where you been, girl?" I don't miss the deep inhale he takes into my hair.

"Oh, being a rebel." I smile, pulling away from him slightly.

"Ah." He grins. "That's not surprising at all."

"No," I answer, ignoring the way everyone in the atrium has silenced. "I guess it's not."

Carter's eyes flick over my shoulder, his smile falling slightly. "Hey, I'll text you."

I inch my head around slightly, not bringing my eyes to the group before looking back at Carter. "Okay, I have the same number." He nods and then yanks me back into his chest again. I exhale. "Hey," I whisper into his chest. He stills, so I take that as he heard me. "Are you all right?"

He releases his breath, so much so that his chest relaxes. He lets go, drawing me back. "I'll text you." His smile stays, but his eyes drop slightly before he turns and walks back out the door.

I stay still, not wanting to turn around and sit back on my seat, because I know that when I do, I'm going to be faced with the Kings. The whispering starts again as all eyes remain glued on me. It's like the first day all over again, only Ally isn't here to fuel the fire. Exhaling, and with a slight eye roll, I turn around, my gaze instantly locking on Bishop. I suck in a deep breath at the way his eyes command mine immediately. Everything ceases to exist whenever he's in the vicinity, which ultimately pisses me off. I hate that I can never control my body whenever he's in the room. Walking toward the boys, I swallow any and all feelings that I have.

Reaching for Nate, I tap his shoulder. "Can I talk to you?" He turns to face me. "Yeah, you okay?"

I pull in my bottom lip and tilt my head, ignoring the glare I'm receiving from Bishop. "Yeah, I think."

"What's wrong?" Nate asks, pushing his hands into his pockets.

I look over his shoulder at the rest of the Kings, and Nate tilts his head over his shoulder and grins. "Sis, these guys know more than you could ever imagine. Anything you have to say to me is fine to say in front of them."

"Yeah," I mutter, looking back to Nate. "For some reason, I have trust issues."

He grins at me slowly. "Well, hell, I wonder why that is. I told Bishop scaring you in the forest was a bad—"

"Nate," Bishop grunts from behind him. "I'll handle it."

I clench my jaw. "No, it's fine. I'm sure Nate has me handled. Thanks."

Bishop wastes no time, stepping toward me, taking hold of my arm, and dragging me out of the atrium. The whispers and chatting stops, and when we reach the entryway, I tug my arm out of his grip.

"What the fuck is your problem, Bishop?" I yell at him, my voice echoing throughout the empty hall. He pushes open the supply closet door and shoves me into the dark room.

"Bishop!" I yell, just as his hand slams over my mouth, pushing me up against the wall.

"Shut up, Madi. What did you want to ask?"

I whack his hand off my mouth. "Can you turn a light on?"

"No."

Exhaling, I lean my head against the wall. "I want to know why no one is asking about Ally."

A long silence drags between us until he finally says, "It's simple. Ally moved away. Anything else?"

So he says Ally moved away and no one questions it? No one questions the Kings? It's like Khales all over again.

"Yes," I scoff, suddenly annoyed at his arrogance. "I wan—"

His chest presses against mine and I slam back against the wall again. Opening my mouth, he cuts me off when his soft lips press against my neck, setting off goose bumps all over my body. Fuck. I really need to find a grip on my feelings when it comes to Bishop, or my plan will turn to shit. I'm taking him down, but I won't complain if he goes down with his face buried between my thighs. May as well enjoy it while it's happening.

"Bishop," I warn, and his mouth kicks up in a grin against my hot flesh. "Bishop," I repeat in the same tone. My eyes close, my breath falling heavily.

"First of all," he growls against my skin, "you don't ask any other questions. You follow ours." His hand skims over my bare thigh and squeezes—enough to leave a bruise. "Second of all, if you want to ask anyone questions," his minty breath now falls over my lips, "you come to me." He pulls my bottom lip into his mouth and bites down on it. He goes to step backward, but I grip the back of his neck and pull him into my lips. He stills, his lips not opening, so I jump up and wrap my legs around his waist.

Stepping forward, he slams me against the wall, his mouth opening to let me in. He groans, tangling his fingers in my hair before yanking it back roughly.

He looks down into my eyes, the faint creak from the door being slightly open lighting the dark room just enough to see him. "What was that about?" I ask.

"What was what about?" he counters, and I tilt my head, studying how his dark jade eyes now look almost black. How his eyebrows pull in, displaying his concentration.

"I don't know," I murmur, looking away. He lets me go, my feet dropping to the floor. Just as he's about to hit the door, I bite my lip. "Bishop!"

"Yeah?" he mutters, turning and looking over his shoulder.

"Why do you like breaking me?"

He smirks slightly, just enough that I see his dimple on the side of his cheek. "Because it gets my dick hard to put you back together."

His response doesn't surprise me, not in the slightest.

"But," I add, stepping forward, "you never put me back together properly. You steal parts of me, so when you do put me back, I'm all crooked, cracked, and still visibly broken."

His smile pauses briefly, not enough for me to really catch any meaning behind it. He turns to face me, his eyes locking onto mine. "Because being broken is how you're going to survive this life, Madison." Then he turns and leaves, the door closing behind him. I remain in the darkness, his words playing on repeat in my brain. What the hell did he actually mean by that?

CHAPTER 10

SHUTTING THE FRONT DOOR AFTER A LONG DAY AT school, I drop my bag on the floor. "Sammy?"

Sammy walks in, wiping her wet hands on the dishtowel she has hanging off her belt. "Ah, Madison!" She whacks me with the back of her hand. "Where the hell have you been?" Shrugging, I go on with the lie my dad has me saying. "I disappeared." Walking into the kitchen, I tug open the fridge and start unloading all the ingredients for grilled cheese. Sammy comes in behind me, leaning against the doorframe.

"Why?" she asks, crossing her arms in front of herself like a worried mother.

"I don't know." Pulling out four slices of bread, I place them on a plate and reach for the butter, swiping it on both sides before slamming some cheese in the middle.

"Who were you with?" she questions in the same tone, eyeing me skeptically.

"Uhh, Tatum. We just traveled a bit. I was mad at Dad for something and didn't feel like coming home. Seriously, Sammy, I'm okay." I put on a completely fake smile for added effect.

Sammy pushes off the doorframe, waving her hands in the air. "*Estúpido jodido adolescente!*"

Flipping my sandwiches, I raise my eyebrows at her retreating back. "Huh? You swearing at me, Sam I am?" I tease, grinning, knowing damn well she can't see me. She's still muttering off in Spanish when Nate walks in, with Bishop following closely behind him. Great, appetite will no doubt be ruined.

"'Sup?" Nate pulls me into him, kissing me softly on the head. "Oh yum." He reaches down and steals a sandwich straight out of the pan. I slap the spatula on the back of his hand, a second too slow because he's already retreating and stuffing his mouth with my delicious creation of carb goodness.

"Screw you, Riverside." I look over my shoulder and sarcastically smile sweetly at Bishop. "Do you want the other one, since I will have to make more anyway." I flip the grilled cheese out and place it on a plate. Walking back toward the middle island, I look up at Bishop when I notice he hasn't answered me. "Hellooo? You want it or not?"

He doesn't answer, just stares.

"You're doing that stare thing again. I thought we were past that phase?" Placing the plate on the counter, I slide it toward him. Ignoring his weird Bishop behavior, I pull out another couple slices of bread and repeat the process.

"Question." Bishop clears his throat.

I look up at him, sucking the cheese off my thumb. "Yes?"

"Don't fucking do that."

"Do what?" I smile around my thumb.

His jaw clenches. "Unless you want to get fucking ru-ined right here with Nate in the next room, I wouldn't do that again."

"Need a better threat than that." I roll my eyes, walking back toward the stovetop and placing my sandwich on the pan. "What was your question?" I turn a little over my shoulder and look at him.

He picks up the grilled cheese and takes a bite. "What do you know about your mom?"

I pause, shuffling around the kitchen to find some paper towels.

"Ahhh, she was my mom?" I answer sarcastically. "I knew all there was to know about her—well, what she would share with me. Why?"

He shakes his head. "Doesn't matter right now."

Rolling my eyes, I finish up my meal and then flip them onto a new plate. Walking toward the bar stool, I slide on top and pick up my food. "So why ask then?"

He shrugs, and just as I'm about to ask another question, Nate walks in with his top off, the shirt tucked into his jeans. "What are we talking about in here?" He grins, sliding onto the stool beside mine.

"Oh, you know, random shit." I take a loud and large bite out of my sandwich. "Oh!" I tap Nate, covering my mouth until I've swallowed my food. "I forgot to ask. Have you heard from Tillie?"

Nate looks around the kitchen. "No? Not since the cabin

deal." Nate hasn't heard from her either? That's weird. I mean, it was weird enough that Ridge hadn't heard from her, but the fact that Nate hasn't got her stashed away somewhere for him to play with whenever he pleases cuts out my idea.

"That's weird." I place my sandwich on my plate.

"Why?" Nate and Bishop both ask at the same time. I reach into my pocket and pull out my phone, tapping on Ridge's number.

"Because Ridge hasn't heard from her either, and she never came home from the cabin."

"That was two months ago," Nate mutters, his eyebrows pulling in.

"Exactly."

"I dropped her off at her house, and yeah, she never texted me back, so I left it," Nate adds, lost in thought.

I hit dial on Ridge's number and bring my phone to my ear.

"Yo!"

"Ridge?"

"Yeah, who's this?"

"Sorry," I murmur, realizing that I never texted him my number. "It's Madison."

"Oh!" He sounds surprised. "Hey."

"Did you ever hear anything back from Tillie?"

"You didn't hear?" he asks in muffled tones. Beeping cars and light chatting fade off in the distance.

"Hear what?" I answer as my heart pounds in my chest. *Please, God, no.*

"She's been a missing person case since. No one has heard from her and no one knows where she is."

"What?" I look up at Nate, who is watching me intently.

He looks worried; I can see it in his eyes. "No one told me anything because I've been out of the country for the past couple of months." I put my phone down and put it on speaker. "You're on speaker phone, and Nate and Bishop are here with me, okay?"

"Yeah, okay," he snickers, though his tone doesn't seem too impressed.

"So can you tell us everything, please?" I urge him, pushing my plate out of the way with my now suddenly lost appetite.

"Well, Nate dropped her off at home after your guys' trip. She stayed for the next couple of weeks but was sick. I went to see her a couple of times, and she was throwing up, pale, and just… sick. Anyway, the last time I saw her, she was acting weird as fuck. She always loved our kick-back sessions."

I look up at Nate, not being able to pass the opportunity. Grinning, I say, "You mean your sex sessions?"

Nate evil-eyes me, flipping me off. I grin deeper.

"Uhh…," Ridge mutters. "Yeah… she told you?" he asks into the phone.

"Yeah, anyway, so what happened?"

Bishop pulls out the bar stool next to me, his thigh brushing mine. I flinch slightly, annoyed at myself once again how much my body sparks to life at his mere proximity, let alone his freaking touch.

"So she rushed me out of the house and then I never heard from her again. Her dad said she left with a suitcase and took his car. They found his car off the interstate a couple of days later, but it was empty with the keys left inside of it. The trail has gone cold and, yeah, again, no one knows where she is. Her cards haven't been used or anything either. She's just gone."

A ball forms in my throat. "Why would she leave?" I whisper, confused. Why would she leave and not even leave a note for anyone? I wouldn't know if she sent me a text because I haven't had my phone, but what is her reasoning?

"Ridge," I start, my brain ticking through ideas. "Who else did she hang with?"

"No one. When it wasn't me, it was you."

"Okay," I murmur. "What do I do?"

"There's not much we can do. I've tried everything. Now all we can do is hope she just comes home."

"Okay. Thanks, Ridge. If I hear of anything, I'll call you. And you do the same?"

"Yeah."

Hanging up, I turn to face Bishop. "What do I do?"

Bishop looks to Nate, and I watch as they both exchange a look. Realization dawns at just who is sitting in front of me.

My face straightens. "I swear to God, if you two have anything to do with this, I will kill you."

"We have nothing to do with this," Nate says, walking toward the sink and filling up a glass with water. He turns to face us, leaning on the counter. "But it's weird as fuck."

"Weird as fuck?" I scoff, getting to my feet. Bishop's hand brushes over my thigh, and I look down at it before looking up at him and then looking back to Nate. "That's an understatement."

"Just leave it for now," Nate tells me, shaking his head. "She obviously doesn't want to be found."

My shoulders slack in defeat. "I guess. But why didn't she come to me if she needed help?"

"Who knows why anyone does anything, Kitty?" Nate

walks up to me, kissing me on the head. "I gotta bounce."

I turn around and watch Nate leave the kitchen before looking to Bishop. "You're not leaving?"

He shakes his head. "No."

"Why?" Honestly, I could do with some time alone.

"I just want to ask you something."

"You always seem to want to ask me something."

He gets to his feet and walks toward me. His chest brushes against mine before his finger comes up and tucks a loose strand of hair behind my ear. "Do you have any memories from when you were young?"

One.

Two.

Three.

Four.

Four.

Four.

"No," I answer, keeping my face straight and my posture stern.

Bishop searches my eyes, his dark green ones daring my secrets to come out. "No."

He leans down, tilts his head, and narrows his eyes. "Are you lying to me, Kitty?"

Lie.

"No."

He pauses, leaving a beat of silence to stretch between us before inching back. "Fine." He steps away and turns to walk out the door. "If you lied to me, I will punish you." Then he's gone, like a fucking tornado whisking up a whole bunch of untouched old emotions. Emotions I have fought hard for years on end to bury. A ten-worded question brought back ten thousand feelings that I have worked so hard to forget. Slamming my eyes shut, I breathe in and out slowly.

In.

Out.

In.

Ou—

"Fuck this." I walk to the liquor cabinet and pull down a bottle of Johnny Walker. Twisting off the cap, I bring the tip to my mouth and swallow. The harsh whiskey hits the back of my throat before slipping down, cloaking all the feelings Bishop raised. Looking down at the bench, an idea pops into my head. I know Elena and Dad have gone away for the week. I grin, taking out my phone. I haven't thrown a party yet, and since Nate has thrown plenty, I think it's time for me to play catch-up. Unlocking my phone, I look at the time quickly. 7:45 p.m. Perfect. I hit dial on Tatum, and she picks up on the second ring.

"Yaaas?"

"Tate?"

"Yes, bitch. What's up?"

"Party at my place."

That perks up her attention. "Oh? When?"

"You come now. The rest can come any time after 10:00 p.m. Spread the word."

"You know I will," she says.

I can just picture her from here, wiggling in her chair with excitement. I take a swig of the whiskey and smirk. "See you soon." Hanging up, I flick my phone between my fingers and listen as the clock ticks loudly in the background. My breathing starts to come in thick, so I take deep intakes of breath and close my eyes.

It's not real. You're here, older, at your house. Home. Safe, warm. It's not real.

One.

Two.

Three.

Four.

Four.

Four.

"Why don't you like me? It's your birthday today. You're supposed to be happy," I whispered toward the mean boy in the sandpit.

"Because you're disgusting. Because you're a life ruiner. Because I fucking hate you."

"That's a bad word," I replied softly, even though I wanted nothing more than to burst into tears. I swallowed past the rejection and handed the boy my shovel anyway.

"I don't fucking want that. Why the fuck do you think I want that now that you've touched it? You're disgusting." He got to his feet, kicking at the sand until the sharp stings cut through my eyes.

"Ouch!" I cried, no longer able to fight the tears as they poured down my cheeks. "What did you do that for?"

"Because I fucking hate you!" the mean boy roared, and then he stormed off back toward his mom.

Why did he hate me? I'd done nothing wrong as far as I knew. The first time I met him was today.

"Brantley!" a woman yelled toward him. "Get here now."

"Hey!" I called out, dusting off the sand from my sundress. "Your name is Brantley?"

"Shut up, freak."

"Madison!" my mom yelled out from the porch. She was

holding a tray of little pirate-shaped cupcakes and wearing a yellow and white sundress. She looked beautiful. I wanted to be as beautiful as her one day. I skipped toward my mom, wiping the tears out of my face. Mommy wouldn't be happy if she saw me crying, and I didn't want to get the boy into trouble. I didn't know why; he was not a very nice boy. I should've wanted to get him into trouble.

"Brantley," my mom said once we both reached her, bending down to my level while still balancing the tray with one hand. "This is Madison." Brantley must've been at least two years older than me. He wore a baseball cap and had an angry scowl on his face. I didn't know why, but I instantly liked him.

"Hi!" I smiled, holding my hand out to him. Maybe if I introduced myself properly, he would like me better. Mommy always said people liked good manners. "I'm Madison. Are these your cupcakes?" I looked up to my mom. "Are these his cupcakes? Is that why they're blue and why I'm not allowed to eat them?" My mom looked at Brantley and me nervously.

"Mom?" I asked again. She was starting to fidget, which she only did when she's nervous.

"Yes, dear. Why don't you and Brantley go play while me and Lucan have a quick word." I must've been confused. Lucan? Bringing my eyes to the new body that stood beside my mom, I looked up the black suit pants, until I finally found ice-cold blue eyes, tanned skin, and blond hair. The man was looking down at me with a dirty stare that made me cuddle into my mom's legs. He kneeled in front of me.

"Well hello. You must be Madison."

I nodded, wrapping my hand in my mom's frilly dress and using it to cover my mouth. "Yes."

"I'm Lucan."

"Hi, Lucan."

He leaned forward, his eyes squinting. "I think I'll call you Silver."

I suck in a breath. Brantley? What the fuck? I remember part of that day now. I recall it so vividly it scares me a little that I didn't remember it until this point. Brantley and I had met? I was at his birthday party? The rest of that day is a little blurry, but there was so much more, because I remember driving home with my mom and dad later that night. So there's still a whole day unaccounted for.

Maybe I could ask my dad.

I frown, grasping the glass bottle. There's no way I can trust my dad with anything now. Can I trust anyone? I know I can trust Tatum, I think, but then again, at one point, I completely trusted my dad. I would have trusted him with my life—and I did on multiple occasions, but yet, he still let me down.

Can I trust anyone?

Can I trust myself?

My brain fuzzes as white noise rings through my ears.

Something has happened. Something has switched inside of me since Bishop asked that question. It has triggered a dark part of my soul I never wanted to acknowledge again.

Have I ever really been safe? Even as a little girl, it seems the adults I trusted and the people I was supposed to be safe with let me down. Feeling more than overwhelmed with my thoughts, I bring the rim of my bottle to my lips, pounding down another couple of mouthfuls until I can't feel the burning sensation in my throat and everything turns numb.

"Trust no one. Fear no one. Fuck everyone," I whisper to

myself, pushing my long hair away from my face. grinning, I walk toward the stairwell and climb up two at a time. I hope Tatum doesn't take too long to get here, but then again—can I really trust her?

Pushing open my bedroom door, a sense of power rushes over me. I trust no one, and that means no one can hurt me. No one can touch me. I'm untouchable because of this revelation. I can't be hurt again. I will fight for my control and my freedom for that little girl. For that broken part of me that yearns for it. Slamming my bedroom door, I take another pull of JW and look toward my closet.

Smirking, I place the bottle on my dresser and make my way to my closet. Flicking on the light, my eyes find my black skinny jeans. They're ripped at the knees and stick to me like a second skin. Grabbing them, I run my fingers over all my crop tops, opting for the most revealing one I can find. A straight across strapless crop top that shows all of my toned stomach. Looking at both items, an idea clicks in my head. Taking the clothes back to my room, I toss them onto my bed and pull open my underwear drawer, taking out my fishnet stockings. Yes, so much yes, this is perfect. Taking everything to my bathroom—and the bottle of my old pal Johnny Walker—I lock Nate's side and my side and turn on the shower. Slipping under the hot cascading water, I take my bottle in with me and sit on the bathtub floor. Hugging the whiskey, I squeeze my eyes closed as the first teardrops. The beading water trickling over my flesh, down my arms like an assault, reminds me of Black Friday's touch.

His rough, aged hands squeezing my nipples tightly.

His rough bearded face scrapping down my delicate chest.

A sob escapes me before I can stop it and I scrub my face angrily. Angry that he's getting tears and hurt so many years later. Bringing the bottle back to my lips, I take a few long pulls of the liquid until I no longer feel like crying. Then I get to my feet and turn off the faucet, the condensation a reminder of my surroundings, bringing me back to the now.

I'm here.

Now.

At home.

Safe.

Safe? Am I? My sanity is because I trust no one. No one will have the power to let me down. I'll expect the worst in people to save disappointment. Wrapping my towel around my body, I quickly dry myself and slip into my little Calvin Klein G-string and then into the fishnet stockings and black jeans. I pull the fishnet waistband up to my ribs so you can see it ripple over my flat stomach and everywhere my jeans are ripped, before sliding on the little crop top boob tube. Smiling down at my outfit, I run the towel through my hair. I look hot and I feel reckless, a toxic combination for me.

I blow out my hair and throw on makeup. Going heavy on the eyes and bright red on the lips. Well, Dad would be proud of the look I have going on right now.

After battling over how to do my hair, I settle on a high messy bun that sits like a bundle of brown curls on the top of my head and grab my bottle. I'm slipping my original Adidas sneakers on when my bedroom door swings open, and Tatum walks in fully dressed in a tight little skirt and heels, clutching a plastic bag in her hand.

"Now, I got Absinth and a couple of kegs," she murmurs, rushing into my room without looking at me. She places the drinks on my bed and finally turns toward me. Her face changes, a small smile creeping onto her mouth. "Well holy shit who fucked on a stick. Where is my friend? And please, don't bring her back."

I roll my eyes and take another drink. "She's gone."

Tate looks impressed. "Well, I like it. Totally digging this look. Carter is downstairs with Ridge starting the music. I hope that's okay, by the way. I saw both of them in town while I was getting alcohol and sort of dragged them with me. But I kind of got the impression you wanted a full house tonight so you wouldn't mind." She adds a cheesy smile.

"Of course I don't mind. A thick bass line starts thumping against the walls as the alcohol warms my blood even more. "I want to dance. Let's go." I pull her toward the door and she pulls back.

"Wait!" She reaches for the plastic bag again and smiles. "Okay, now I'm ready!"

We pound down the stairs, me with my bottle of whiskey clutched between my fingers and Tatum swinging the plastic bag. Hitting the bottom of the stairwell, Carter whistles at us, a mischievous grin on his face.

"Damn, mami…."

"Hey!" I smile. He pulls me in for a hug, and I slouch into him, my muscles slightly relaxing for the first time since this afternoon. Inching back, he pushes a couple of loose strands away from my face and smiles his boyish grin.

Pressing back softly, I look over his shoulder at Ridge, who looks like he has almost finished setting up the little makeshift DJ booth area in the sitting room. I point to the floor-to-ceiling doors and nudge my head at Tatum. "Open up the doors and turn on the Jacuzzi and pool lights. Tonight is going to be a long night."

"Long night, huh?" Tatum wiggles her ass, sliding open the doors. "Well, as long as I get fucked, I don't care."

"All class, Sinclaire," Carter murmurs.

Tatum flips him off. "Never claimed to be classy, Mathers."

I roll my eyes, leaving the two to banter between each other and making my way toward Ridge. "Hey!"

He looks over his shoulder, putting all the wires and cords back into the little black boxes.

"Hey, Madi. Hope it's okay. Your friend," he looks over at Tatum, "is a little persistent. Anyway, she somehow knew I DJ'd at one of the underage clubs in town, so here I am."

I laugh, not surprised that Tatum knew that information about Ridge. She probably knows his address, birthplace, birthdate, and blood type too. "No, please, you're doing us a favor. It was sort of an impulse idea."

Ridge chuckles, walking behind the DJ setup and putting on his headphones. "The best nights start with that line right there."

"I hope so." I smile at him and tilt my head. He's cute, in a boy-raised-on-the-wrong-side-of-the-tracks kind of way. He has a sort of swagger to him that makes him even more appealing.

"Sorry about her." I laugh, looking toward Tatum, who has opened out the ranch slider doors. "She's a little—"

"Intrusive?" Ridge interrupts, smirking at me.

I laugh, my eyes locking with his. "Yeah, I guess you could say that. But she means well."

"Yeah." Ridge winks, his arm wrapping around my waist as he pulls me into him. "So tell me—"

"No," I cut him off, looking up at him. "I don't want to answer any questions tonight." I bring my hands up to his chest and press lightly. "I just want to forget everything." He steps back and searches my eyes.

"Everything okay?"

Smiling, I nod. "Yeah, everything's fine." He turns back to the DJ deck and flicks on some sort of remixed, hard, house song, and I turn around, finding Tatum straight away. She wiggles her eyebrows at me suggestively, and I roll my eyes. I swear, only Tatum would take me talking to a guy the completely wrong way. Walking up to her, I squint my eyes. "What?"

"Oh, nothing." She grins, dancing around in a circle just as the doorbell rings. "Oh look, the party is here!"

I smile, shaking my head and taking a long pull of the whiskey again, relishing how it numbs everything inside of me, physically and mentally. The more I drink, the more I forget. With that thought, I take another sip just as the song changes to "Where the Girls At" by David Guetta. Tatum lifts her drink in the air, and with a whole bunch of people walking in behind her, she screams, "Let's get fucked up!" at the top of her lungs.

I raise my bottle in the air in salute, grinning at her. Spinning around, I start dancing in the middle of the floor, grinding and pressing against the sea of bodies. The song changes to "No Promises" by Cheat Codes and I spin around, lost in the numb feeling the whiskey has given me.

Until my eyes lock onto Bishop, who is standing in the entryway of the sitting room with Nate and the rest of the Kings in formation behind him.

Bishop's scowl deepens when he sees someone rubbing

up behind me. Rolling my eyes, I walk toward them, an innocent smile on my face. "Hi, boys!"

"Madison!" Nate snaps at me. "What the fuck?"

"What?" I slur, my head swimming in a deep pool of whiskey. "Like I can't throw a party, what?" I laugh sarcastically. "I'm not Nate Riverside." Nate grabs my arm, but I yank it away from him. "Screw you, all of you. Leave me the fuck alone." Then I push through them and make my way toward the kitchen. Leaning down into the cabinet, I pull out a glass and fill it up with water. Turning around, I find Bishop leaning against the doorframe, arms crossed in front of him.

"Why throw the party, Madison?"

"Why not, Bishop?" I retort, matching his tone. I tip my water out and go to walk out the door, only his hand catches my arm.

"Why you acting out?"

I pull my arm out of his grip. "Why don't you mind your fucking business?" Then I walk back onto the dance floor, snatching a bottle of whatever the fuck it is out of someone's hands. Cisco Kid from Redman starts pumping through the speakers, and I let go. Dancing and riding the beat, I grind up on the closest person near me. Turning around and wrapping my arms around his neck, I bring my eyes to—

"Brantley?" I go to pull away, but he grips onto my arms, locking me there.

"Nah-uh, you ain't going anywhere. You don't grind up on a man's dick like that and expect to walk away."

I narrow my eyes, the room spinning. "I can do what the fuck I want."

He laughs, a menacing chuckle that vibrates against my chest—a tone I know I should run from, because this is freaking Brantley. Though Bishop is just as terrifying as Brantley—if not worse—I know Bishop on a level I don't know Brantley. I know how far I can push Bishop for him to not hurt me. Do I think he could still hurt me and probably would if I push him far enough? Abso-fucking-lutely.

I search Brantley's eyes, lost in the music and intoxicated by whiskey. I lean my body into his a bit more and bring my hands down his sharp jawline, running my index finger over the bottom of his plump lip. He catches my index finger between his teeth, and I give him a menacing grin. Wrapping his lips around my finger, he unlatches his teeth and sucks on my finger; it comes out of his mouth with a pop. Closing my eyes, I ignore the way my nipples are pushing against the cups of my bra, or the way my flesh has come alive.

Before I know what I'm doing, I come up on my tippy toes and kiss him. He opens his mouth, letting my tongue in as his arm hooks around my bare waist and his finger dips into the band of my fishnet tights, flicking at it. I lick his tongue, pulling on it slightly before he bites down on my lower lip. Pulling back, I bring my nose to his and search his eyes. His eyes that are lit with lust—dark, domineering, and powerful lust. Do I dance on this line? This dangerous line of something I know I could never come back from?

Yes.

"Go upstairs?" I whisper against his lips.

He smirks, the curve of his mouth pressing against mine. His dimple pops out and I groan like an unhinged horny teenager.

"Naw, babe. That's too mainstream for me." He takes my hand and tugs me toward the open doors. "Come." I take another drink and go to place it on the countertop, only for him to pick it back up. "We're gonna need this."

We pass Tatum briefly near the stairwell, and she looks at me, eyes wide. "What the fuck?" she mouths, shock evident on her face.

I shrug and follow Brantley anyway. Stepping outside, he pulls me again, tucking me under his arm and leading me toward his RT Dodge Charger. I pull open the passenger side and slip into the dark leather seats. The car is nice, sort of looks like the one Vin Diesel drives in *The Fast and the Furious*. Brantley gets into the driver seat and roars her to life, the deep V8 engine vibrating underneath me.

"Where we going?" I ask, turning to face him.

He smirks. "You have no idea." Then he floors it out of the driveway. As we pass all the streetlights and overgrown trees, I begin to sober a little. "Brantley?" I whisper as he drops it down to second gear and accelerates. I look toward him. "Brantley, where are we going?" His face straightens, all playfulness that I saw earlier gone. That's when realization sinks in. I just got into a car with Brantley—thinking I was going to fuck the shit out of him, only now I'm fearing for my life. I've made a lot of mistakes in my life, but I have a feeling this one is going to take the cake. My phone vibrates in my back pocket, and I sit up, pulling it out and opening the message from an unknown number.

Riddle me this...

CHAPTER 11

FUCK!

I look toward Brantley. "What the fuck is this?"

Brantley laughs and floors it forward. "As I said— you have no idea."

Slamming my eyes shut, I squeeze my phone in my hand, ignoring the text and not wanting to read on. Brantley must sense this because he decides to take over.

"Riddle me this, Kitty. What happens when you drink from poison, thinking it's love, but when you get hit with the buzz, things start to fuzz, until you can't breathe, and your suffocating becomes the release?"

Fear prickles over my skin and I shake my head. "Nate said he was done fucking with me. Bishop wouldn't do this to m—"

"Oh, but he would. You see…" Brantley grins, dropping

gears and driving us onto the highway. "Human emotions are a fickle thing. They can blind even the smartest of people and make them think that someone won't do bad, but people will always do bad. There's no stopping that. So tell me, Madison." He looks at me now as he applies more pressure on the accelerator.

"Brantley, your speed."

His eyes stay on mine, the darkness of them sucking me in like sinking sand. "Don't care. But tell me," his smirk deepens as he puts his attention back to the road ahead of him, "what makes you think Bishop really gives a fuck about you?"

"He does, a little bit," I murmur, realizing how deluded I must sound. This is Bishop Vincent Hayes—king of no emotions and zero fucks given. Why am I cocky enough to declare he gives more than a fuck about me?

Brantley laughs. "Oh, Madison. There's so much you don't know, and won't know. But one thing you should know is that Bishop has no feelings for anyone. He plays the game right, draws them in enough to think he gives a fuck, but ultimately, he doesn't. There's a reason why he's the king of the Kings, Kitty, and it's not because of his overwhelming river of feels he pours upon girls. It's because he ends lives without flinching."

I swallow past the ball of fear that has developed in my throat. "You won't win this round, Brantley." I look at him, really regretting the alcohol consumption and inwardly declaring I will never drink like this again.

"Naw, Kitty." Brantley grins again, pulling down a long dark road. "We've already won." Then he slides into the driveway and floors it until we reach the cabin we all stayed at months ago. Memories come flooding back, and I realize how naïve I've been when it comes to Bishop and Nate. I was deluded with the idea of loyalty, when in fact that didn't mean anything to them. Never did. They warned me that I was just a pawn in their game—I move when they want me to move, speak when they want me to speak. I just didn't realize it until now.

"What do you want?" I ask, my tone flat. "You guys give me whiplash with these games."

Brantley smirks and then gets out of the car, walking around to my side, and then yanks it open. "Get the fuck out."

"No!" I snap back at him, and he reaches inside, pulling me out by the arm. "Let me go!" I scream at him, only it falls on deaf ears, because he grabs me by the back of my neck and starts tugging me toward the front door. The bright headlights from the car beam on the modern log cabin I had been to what feels like not that long ago. Bringing my hand up to my forehead to shade from the bright light, just as we hit the bottom step, the car revs behind us and I spin around, catching Brantley grinning. His other hand lets go of my arm as he puts a cigarette between his lips, sparking it to life. Looking back to the car in confusion, a light shines from inside of the car, displaying long black hair. Who the hell is that? She looks right at me and smirks, but even from here I can tell she's beautiful. Exotic-looking, but beautiful. She turns to look over her shoulder and floors it backward before spinning and driving down the long driveway.

"What is this?" I ask out loud, my eyes and focus remaining on the fading headlights. When Brantley doesn't answer back, I turn to ask him, "Brant—" Only he's gone. I spin around a full 360, trying to find where he disappeared to. "Brantley!" I growl. "This is not funny!" The temperature suddenly drops, thick fog slipping out of my mouth between each word. Figuring he's definitely not coming back, I run my hands up and down my arms, rubbing the goose bumps off my flesh. Taking the front steps carefully because I can't see shit, I feel around for the railing. Opening and closing my eyes, they slowly begin to adapt to the surroundings, but not enough for me to really see what I'm doing.

"Shit!" I mutter under my breath, grabbing my phone from my back pocket. I quickly slide it open and go to press Call on Tatum when I see the service bars keep dropping in and out. "Motherfucker." Using the light from my phone, I aim it toward the front door and grab onto the handle, wiggling it but it doesn't unlock. Giving up, I start walking along the wraparound porch when my phone goes off. Swiping my phone open, I read the message.

Run.

An overwhelming sense of terror rushes over me. I spin around suddenly, finding no one there. Nothing but my damn imagination. I know these boys play games—this isn't my first rodeo with them—but the thing I don't know is how far they'll push it. I've seen Bishop kill three people now. I'm not about to play Russian roulette with my life and in the hands of a psychopathic billionaire, or whatever the fuck he is.

"I'm not playing your games!" I yell into the dark night. Waiting for a reply, or even a laugh, I hear... nothing. The mere whisks of wind brushing through the dry almost-autumn leaves is all that replies. Swallowing past my fear, I walk along the porch more, remembering the back door. Maybe Brantley just left me here as a sick joke. It wouldn't surprise me if that was his stupid plan. Rolling my eyes, I walk farther until I get to the side door that's tucked behind the kitchen.

Wiggling the door handle, but it's locked too. I turn around, banging the back of my head against the door. "Fuck," I murmur. Rustling leaves catch my attention, and I whip my head toward it. "Brantley!" I snap. "This isn't funny. We can leave now! You've made your point."

"A little cocky for a chick who hasn't been on the scene for too long, don't ya think?"

I know that voice all too well.

"Well, how not surprising it is to see you come out of the shadows, Bishop. Take me home. It's cold." I push off the door and go to walk past him, only his hand flies up to my arm and he pushes me backward. The back of my head smashes against the door. "Fuck! You—"

His hand slams over my mouth while his free one clenches over my throat. He squeezes tight, enough to have my head pulsing with the lack of oxygen. I tap on his arm, looking deep into his eyes. I'm barely able to make out his sharp eyes and jaw in the dark. His lip curls in a devious grin that makes me both weak in the knees and in the head, because that grin should really put the fear of God into me—and it does. But it also has my stupid lady bits tingling.

"Cut the fucking shit, Madison. What the fuck is with you tonight, and only answer me honestly." He tilts his head, dragging his eyes up and down my clothing. "Remember that game we played in the forest?" He unlatches his grip from my throat and releases my mouth, stepping back slightly. Pulling out an army knife from his back pocket, he flicks it open and then in a flash the blade is pressing into my neck, and his hand is back, covering my mouth. He runs his nose over mine, searching my eyes. "Mmmm." He smirks, his deep growl vibrating over my chest. "You're distracting."

"Nothing is wrong," I snap when he releases my mouth slightly. I keep my head up, staring at his eyes as he glares back at mine in challenge. "Let me go."

He slams me up against the wall again, the knife still pressed against my neck and his knee coming between my legs. He presses his leg against my clit, and my eyes close, but the knife running down my collarbone sets off electrical currents that have my senses working on overtime. I'm so fucked with Bishop. How can we be so attracted to each other—unwillingly—but hate each other all the same? My eyes pop open when he slices the middle of my strapless crop top, my nipples aching as the cool night air licks over them, igniting them to life. *Focus, Madison. Focus.*

"Stop fucking lying to me, Madison!" Bishop yells, getting more up in my face. Bringing both arms to either side of my head, he cages me in. "Why. The fuck. Did me questioning your past today trigger something with you? Hmm?" he asks, grinding his thickness against my tummy.

Fight it.

"It didn't."

"Tell me the truth, Madison."

Lie.

"It triggered nothing."

Bishop brings the knife back down and runs the blunt side of it over my nipple. I suck in a breath and hold. *One second. Two seconds. Three seconds.* My body's will to breathe wins and I exhale just as the blade comes down to my jeans. He cuts the waistband to my fishnets, and it springs loose, hanging over the top of my jeans.

"One more time, Madison, or I'm going to fuck you with this knife and lick your blood clean off as you watch."

I close my eyes. "Not—"

He launches his fist into the wall beside my face. I've never seen Bishop so out of control, and I don't know why it's my reaction to my past that has set him off—but it has. Set. Him. Off. "Stop fucking lying!"

Clenching my eyes closed, I take in a few deep breaths. Don't walk down that aisle. Don't do it... don—

Walking down the blood-red hall, Madison squeezed the man's hand. "Where are you taking me?"

"You'll see, Silver. You'll see."

"Will there be any other kids there to play with?"

The man looked down to Madison and grinned. "You'll see."

"No!" I rock back and forth on the concrete in front of the door, cradling my knees up to my chest. Tears pour down my cheeks and sweat beads my skin regardless of the fact I'm sitting in the brisk cool night with absolutely no shirt on. "No, no, no..." Shaking my head, I can still hear his voice in the back of my consciousness. "It's just a dream. It's just a bad dream. He won't come back," I repeat, rocking back and forth and fisting my hair.

"Madison, Madison! Fuck!"

Whose voice is that?

"No!" I shake my head again, lost in my dark abyss of bleeding memories. "He always comes back."

"Madison!" another voice roars in the background. A different voice.

"Come back, baby."

I know *that* voice.

My eyes spring open, a blood-curdling scream ripping out of my chest. "Don't fucking touch me!" Consciousness starts to seep in, and I look up to see Bishop, Nate, Hunter, Brantley, Cash, Eli, and Chase circling me. I cover my front right away, and Bishop rips off his hoodie, pushing it over my head before tucking his arms under my legs and lifting me off the ground. I snuggle into his chest, inhaling his spicy, sweet scent.

"What, what did I say?" I murmur through sobs.

"You said enough for us to know enough." Bishop's jaw tenses as he looks directly at Nate, who still hasn't looked at me.

"Nate?" I whisper, but he doesn't acknowledge me. His eyes stay locked on Bishop's. A wave of humiliation washes over me. Is he ashamed of me? That this happened to me? Does he look at me differently now? All my worst fears come crashing into my chest like a freight train. I'm dirty. No one can love something or someone who has been through what I have. His knowing what I've been through has now tainted what he thought of me; I just know it. My heart snaps in my chest and my throat swells as tears start to pour down my cheeks again.

"Take her home," Nate replies emotionlessly.

"Nate?" I try again through a broken throat. "Talk to me."

He doesn't move, keeping his eyes on Bishop. "Take her home."

Bishop's grip tightens around me. "We'll talk about this later," he warns Nate.

I don't see Nate's reaction, because I've buried my head into the crook of Bishop's neck, his pulse pounding against my nose. Putting me in the passenger seat, Bishop shuts the door and then comes to his side, sliding in and firing up his Maserati.

"Madi, we don't have to talk about anything right now, but eventually, I want to know 100 percent of what happened and everything in between—okay?"

I don't say anything, watching how the dark night dances between the tree branches and leaves.

"Answer me."

"Yes," I reply. "I'll tell you everything I remember."

He floors it forward as we leave the cabin in the distance.

"Why?" I croak out once we hit the highway.

"Why, what?" He looks to me every couple of seconds while still keeping his eyes ahead on the road.

"Why did you have to do it this way. Why scare me?"

He pauses briefly until the silence stretches out. "Fear is your patch, babe. We all have our patches. Those little spaces that could bring us to our knees if dabbled with."

The answer surprises me. "Oh, and what's yours?"

He pauses again, long enough for me to guess he's not going to answer, so I lean my forehead on the cool window and close my eyes, suddenly feeling tired and drained.

"You."

My eyes snap open. Not wanting to be overly obvious about how surprised I am, I keep my eyes locked on the dark road ahead. "What?"

"I didn't have one," Bishop confesses. "It's how my father raised me, why I am who I am. Our blood, I mean, who we are, we can't afford to have a patch. My dad doesn't have one either. He married my mom for a cover, not for love—not that I'm talking about love." He looks toward me to enhance his point then focuses back on the road. "But I'm just saying, I can't have one. The fucking feelings I get when I think some-one is fucking with you, though?" He breathes out a gush of air. "I'd kill them in an instant and not think twice about doing it. That may not be because I caught feelings for you or anything like that. It could just be because we're sort of… friends. In a fucked way."

"Friends?" I mimic, trying that word on my tongue. So he's overprotective of me and has some sort of feelings for me. If not, then why would he kill someone over me? He sounds confused, about as confused as I am about him. I get where he's coming from, Bishop has always been different for me too, regardless of whatever fucked shit he put me through. Is that really dangerous for him though? To feel that strongly about a "friend?"

"Why is that a bad thing?" I quickly ask before I can stop myself. "I mean, why is having a patch a bad thing?"

"It's a weakness. I had nothing to lose until I met you. I can't afford to have a weakness, not in this lifetime."

"Well maybe we'll meet each other in another lifetime, and I can be more than a patch to you." I glance at him, and his eyes lock onto mine. The dark depths sink into mine, clinging like a flame does to embers.

"And what would that be?" he asks, his brows pulling in as he looks from my mouth to my eyes.

"Yours."

Pulling up to my house, Bishop gets out of the driver side and opens my door.

"I can walk, Bishop."

"Yeah," he murmurs, scooping his arms under my legs and lifting me from my seat. "But you don't have to." After our brief talk on the way home, I've realized I need to let him go. I can't keep holding on to whatever it is I think we could have together, because it's not going to happen. He's Bishop Vincent Hayes, and I'm me. A fucking mess.

I turn my face to him just as we reach the front door. The front door that is showing no display of the house party that was raging earlier. I guess someone—or some King—shut it down. "Can I ask you something?"

He opens the door wide. "Yeah."

"If I ask you something... will you tell me the truth?"

"That depends," he answers, walking inside and closing the door behind us. "If it's about me, then yes, but if it's about the club, then no."

"Loyalty?" He puts me down and I make my way upstairs with him following behind.

"Something like that," he mutters under his breath. It's so quiet I almost miss it. Walking into my room, I stretch out on my bed, blowing my hair out of my face. The mattress dips where Bishop takes a seat. "I need to ask you something, and I need you to be honest with me," he begins.

I swallow down any nerves those words raised, and nod. I know what he's going to ask, and I've been mentally preparing myself for it the whole way home, but it's still unsettling me. I've never said the words out loud. I've never told anyone my darkest secret, let alone a guy I have feelings for.

"Did someone do something to you when you were little?"

Turning toward him, I prop my head up onto the palm of my hand. The shadows from the dim lamp cast sharp lines over his jaw and perfect nose. He has the profile of a GQ model, but the twisted mind of Michael Myers. Ahh, charming.

Exhaling, I close my eyes. "Yes."

He grits his teeth, and I open my eyes and watch as his hands ball into fists on top of his knees. His nostrils flare. "Who?"

I know his name. I don't know where he is or what happened to him, but I know his name.

"I don't know who he is. I don't remember much of it. All I know is it started when I was young." I lie on my back and bring my hands under my head.

"Give me any details you can," Bishop urges, turning to face me. "I mean it, Madison."

Oh, I know he means it, and I know if I give him the name, he will have no problem finding this guy. It doesn't matter if Lucan is in China or if he's six feet under already. I know Bishop will find him, and he will kill him if he's still alive, but that's *my* kill. I promised myself long ago that one day I will get my retribution, and I'm not about to cheat my younger self out of that promise, so I lie. "I don't know his name."

Bishop studies my face closely, and I start to panic. I know he can read people; he reads people so accurately, but he has always said how he struggles to read me. Even though I know this, paranoia kicks into overtime, and I clear my throat, knowing I have to give him something so he can back off a little. Bishop opens his mouth, probably about to call me out on my obvious lie, but I interject. "He would call me Silver."

"Silver?" Bishop asks, thinking over those words. "What, like as in he knew you were the Silver Swan?"

I shrug. "I honestly don't know."

Bishop gets up and walks toward the door. Pausing, he

inches his head over his shoulder. "Get some sleep." Then he walks out and leaves me there brewing. Shit. Did I give too much? Has he worked out who that is? Surely not. No one knew that was what Lucan called me except me and Lucan… and….

Forget.

But Bishop is smart—too smart. He picks up things that slip past normal ears and eyes.

Swinging my legs off the bed, I reach underneath until my hand skims over the worn leather I've become so accustomed to touching. Pulling it out, I shuffle up my bed until I'm leaning against the headboard. Flipping open the first few pages, I jump to where I was up to.

10.

Revelation

Et delicatis praetulissem, sicut truncum arboris fluitantem olor et quasi argentum bullet sicut mortiferum.

- *As alluring as a floating swan, but as deadly as a silver bullet.*

"*I want to know why,*" *I probed, trying to get Humphrey to confess. Why is it so important that a woman is not to be born into this cult?*

"*I told you, woman. You only know what I want you to know. None of this has to make sense to you, because you're a woman.*" *Biting down every reaction I had, I took a seat on one of the chairs. Gazing into the scalding hot flame that flicked up to the stone fireplace, I whipped my head toward him.*

"*Tell me.*" *Deciding I was going to fight him on this, I got up off my chair and walked toward him. "I want to know. I have a right to know—my..." I stopped, the swelling of my throat halting any and every movement.*

One.

Two.

Three.

I began counting internally, ordering the tears to sink back into their sockets.

Humphrey rose up off his chair and headed toward me. His expression changed, all the lines and wrinkles that carved through his face deepened, and that's when I knew I had struck a nerve. I always did. He reared his hand back and slapped me across the cheek, the sting causing a rush of heat to flame up my face. I fell to the ground in a heap, holding the throbbing ache and looking up at him.

He kneeled down beside me. "Now, I'm going to tell you a little something, not because you asked, or rather, demanded, but because I want to. Understand me?"

I nodded, because I had no other choice if I wanted to see the sunrise tomorrow or my son again.

He inched toward me, his breath heating my earlobe. I shivered in disgust, but hid it, knowing rightly that him becoming aware of the fact he disgusts me would warrant me another beating. "Because women can't be trusted. Because women are easily distracted by fame and money. Because the amount of power the Silver Swan could gain would be immense, because that thing between your legs is a weakness. A patch. It's alluring, and it's distracting."

"So you do this because she would have too much power?"

"Ahhh," Humphrey grinned, "she gets it. Yes, she would also be too appealing to the other Kings. Far, far too appealing.

There's no way, and that is why we can never have a Silver Swan. As alluring as a peaceful swan floating on water, but as lethal as a silver bullet."

"What if, in generations of times from now, one slips through the cracks?" I asked, genuinely concerned for the future Swan, as there was a high chance there will be plenty. But whether any survive will be a different story. I do hope someone in this cult shows compassion at one point and saves her.

"Then she will grow to wish she was never born."

"Well, you got that right, fucker," I murmur, closing the book and sliding it back under my bed. I sure do fucking wish I was never born sometimes, but what did he mean by that? Why was he so sure that if any of them made it out alive, they would wish they were never born? I could say it was just Humphrey and his cocky character, but something about his certainty throws me off. My head pounds, reminding me of my long night, and I slide off the bed, dragging my overly tired ass to the bathroom.

Turning on the faucet, I wait for the water to warm up to a scalding heat and slide in. Squeezing some shampoo into the palm of my hand, I throw it into my hair and scrub, letting the soapsuds rain over my skin. I'm lost in thoughts of the latest finding in *The Book* when the bathroom door swings open, and the curtain gets ripped away, revealing Nate standing there, no shirt on with gray sweat pants.

"Nate!" I scream, covering my private bits. "Get the fuck out!"

He doesn't say anything, his pupils are dilated, and his chest is heaving as he takes in deep breaths.

"Have you been running?" I ask, totally off subject but

finally noticing the glistening of sweat covering his skin. Reaching for my towel, I still keep my eyes locked on his to make sure he doesn't cop a look, but he doesn't. He just stares at me, his eyes looking between each of mine intently, like he's searching for something important. Answers, maybe, answers I can't give him.

"Nate!" I repeat when the awkward silence gets too much. Grasping the towel, I quickly wrap it around myself. Feeling more secure now that I'm not butt-naked, I reach up and touch the side of his cheek. "What's wrong?" I care about Nate, I do. More than I like to admit it, but I do. I've always had an inkling of feelings for him deep down, and though I squash them and bring it down to him being my brother, I can't help it. My heart aches when his does and beats when he's happy. Whether that's what usually happens when you have a brother, I don't know—I wouldn't know. The feelings are new to me, so I'm still trying to work them out.

His eyes close once my palm touches his cheek, a small breath hissing between his teeth. His abs tense, every muscle in his body looking overworked. "Nate?" I whisper again, getting out of the shower so my body is flush up against his. He's almost a good foot taller than me, so I look up to him. "Talk to me."

He wraps his arm around my back and pulls me into his chest. Reaching down, he brushes off a few strands of hair that were stuck to my face. "I… can't—fuck!" He lashes out at the end. "Who?"

"Who what?" I answer, even though I know I'm playing with fire. I've not seen Nate quite this dark before, and though it's terrifying, I know with more certainty than I do about Bishop that he would never hurt me.

"Don't." His voice is sharp, full of dominance. That simple word twisting my heart into two.

"I told Bishop I don't know his name. All I know is that he called me Silver."

Nate tilts his head, his eyebrows pulling in as the wheels start to turn in his head. "Silver?" His other arm comes behind me so he has me locked in both now. "As in the Silver Swan? As in he's a motherfucking King?"

"I don't know what he is or who he is, Nate. I don't want to talk about this anymore."

That sobers him a little, his features relaxing for the first time since he stormed in here. "You know," I murmur, wrapping my hands around the back of his neck, "one of these days you're going to need to stop storming into the bathroom while I'm showering."

The corner of his mouth kicks up in a small smirk, showing one of his dimples. "Yeah, I guess one of these days I will. But not today, or tomorrow, or even next month." The cushion of his thumb traces along the bottom of my lip. His eyes zone in on the motion, and in the back of my brain, I know what's about to happen.

My breathing shallows, my chest constricting. I want to make him feel better. I hate that he's so worked up over something that has to do with me. Something he shouldn't feel worked up over because I buried it long ago. Closing my eyes, I inch up on my tippy toes and press my lips to his. He stills at first. A couple of seconds pass, and he still hasn't relaxed, so I go to pull away, only his hand comes to the back of my neck, stopping me. He pushes my lips into his more and opens slightly, his tongue licking across my bottom lip. My stomach flips, my flesh sparking to life from the connection, and I pull him in more. Our kissing turns hot and needy, and in a second, he's whipped the towel from my body, his hands gripping around the back of my thighs and lifting me off my feet.

"Fuck!" He pauses, catching his breath. I count to five in my head, attempting to slow my erratic breathing—and hormones. Closing my eyes, he leans his forehead against the wall beside my head, my sex pressing against his stomach and my legs still wrapped around his waist.

"We can't do this—and I can't fucking believe I just said that, because God fucking knows I want this with you, Mads." He places soft kisses on my collarbone.

"How long?" I whisper out.

"How long what?" he replies, his lips brushing over my shoulder and his lip ring leaving a cool sensation in its wake.

"How long have you been in love with me?"

He pauses and squeezes me tightly. "Longer than you know."

I pull in a breath. "Nate," I warn. "I know I feel something for you too. I mean, I always have. And I've always fought it—but love? I mean I love you. I love you so very much, but *in* love? That's not something I know."

He steps back, placing me back down to my feet slowly and picking up my towel again, wrapping it around my body. He tightens the front and smiles a sweet smile that doesn't reach his eyes. Placing a small kiss on my forehead, he whispers, "I know." Then he walks out the bathroom and into his bedroom, and just like that, everything is back to normal.

Did I just imagine that? He came into my bathroom like a tornado, leaving a massacre of feelings behind. Fucking Nate Riverside. Fucker. But I love that fucker, very much, but if I were to compare the two feelings—Nate and Bishop— they're oh so different. Both intense, but incredibly different. Now I've just got to figure out what means what. Like a love puzzle of mass destruction, only we don't know who will pull the trigger. I slide under my sheets, and then twist and turn for hours until I finally get some sleep.

I got shit for sleep last night, and I haven't been able to stomach any food all morning. The hangover of doom awaited me with the sun this morning, and now I don't want to live, let alone adult. Throwing on some sweatpants and a loose white tee, I walk downstairs, twisting my hair up into a messy bun.

"Morning, sweetheart," Elena greets. She's chopping up all sorts of fruit and putting them into the blender to make one of her godawful smoothies.

"Morning." I, on the other hand, head straight for the pot of coffee, praising the gods when I see it's full.

"Sleep well?" she asks, putting the lid on the blender and unleashing hell upon my ears.

"Actually," I yell over her intrusion that comes compacted in green slime. "I slept like shit!" I yell, only she cut off the blender just in time that I didn't just yell; I sort of screamed.

"Wow." Nate grins, walking into the kitchen with dark sweatpants and no shirt on. I quickly avert my eyes, guilt washing over me as I think back to what happened between us last night. "I would have thought you slept like a baby, sis." Instantly, I cut my eyes to his and growl under my breath. He did not just "sis" me after we were seconds away from doing the deed not long ago.

"Well, I didn't," I snap at him, sipping on my coffee and

making my way to one of the barstools.

"Oh, well that's unfortunate." Elena bounces around the kitchen in her running gear, slurping on her green juice. "I have some flaxseed oil that might help you with sleeping, Madison. It has a good history, and—"

"Thanks," I interrupt. Usually I'm not so rude, but I have a pounding headache from Hades, and horns are starting to grow out of my head. "I'll keep that in mind." I offer her a little smile, leaning on my elbows and massaging my temples. Elena walks out, leaving Nate and me together in the kitchen alone.

"You all right?" He grins at me, leaning against the counter and sipping on a mug of coffee. Something so natural but looks way too smoking coming from Nate. I need to get out of here.

"Fine!" I clear my throat, standing to my feet.

"Where you going?" he yells from behind me as I take the first step upstairs.

"Going to shoot shit."

CHAPTER 12

A
FTER I'VE PACKED UP MY GUNS, I LOAD THEM INTO
the back of the Range Rover and slip into the driver
seat before making my way to the area my dad and
I used to shoot when I was a kid. I remember it vaguely, and
it's a bit of a drive away, but I need some time away from
my house and everyone in my life. I'm starting to get cabin
fever, or people fever, so I think hiding out where I have good
memories as a kid is the best way to ground myself again.

I get into NYC later that evening and my phone has been
ringing nonstop. None from my dad, just from Nate and
Tatum, and even a few from Bishop. They won't understand
my need to get away—no one ever does. I love my friends—
and whatever the hell the Kings are—but I'm not about to
pour my life story to them and drop all the walls I spent years
upon years building. I like to think I'm smarter than that.

Pulling into the old ranch, I make my way down the gravel drive, the trees and gardens all immaculately groomed and trimmed. I don't remember it being this impeccable, but then again, I was all of ten the last time I was here.

I pull up to the front entrance and the valet comes to my door.

"Name?" he asks, the brim of his hat hiding his young features.

"Oh, um, I haven't made a reservation. Do I need to?" I look around, taking in the rich scale and vast size of the place. It screams elite; of course I need a reservation.

"Yes, I apologize, ma'am." He speaks English, but he doesn't sound American.

"Oh!" I act surprised. "That's okay."

I'm just about to close the door when a woman's voice stops me. "Excuse me!" she interrupts from the main entrance. "Madison? Montgomery?" I look her up and down, not sure whether I should respond or drive off. How could she know my name?

The young boy stills, his jaw tensing.

"Uhh." I internally battle with how to answer. Looking at her again, I notice how she's dressed immaculately. Tight black pencil skirt, blood-red silk blouse, dark hair pinned up in a tight high ponytail, sharp stilettos. Oh yeah, this woman oozes power and money.

"Yeah?" My brain-to-mouth filter malfunctions, because I sure as fuck did not authorize that answer.

"She doesn't need a reservation." The woman floats down the marble steps and makes her way toward us.

"I don't?" I reply, confusion no doubt evident on my face.

"No, honey." She smiles, taking my hand. "Come on in. I'll get the keys to your room." She must know my father; that's the only explanation I have. Because how else would she know my name and who I am?

Looking over my shoulder at the young valet, his face is tilted toward the ground, his expressions not visible from where I'm walking. When he looks back to me, his eyes catch mine like a magnet, and I instantly feel a strange sense of familiarity with him. His eyes are milk chocolate, his skin pale, his cheekbones are high and defined, and his jaw is angular. From what I can tell, he can't be older than sixteen, maybe seventeen—he's young. His body isn't very large either; it's more of a lean stature.

Bringing my attention back to where I'm going, the woman walks through the main glass doors and pauses at the threshold, gesturing for me to enter. Taking this moment to case out the place, I grip onto my shoulder strap and look around uneasily. The place looks the same from my memory, maybe a few things being upgraded, but the concept of the ranch remains the same. Rich, old, and classy. It's situated on the outskirts of New York, deep in the woods. My father would tell me this was a safe place where we could go shooting in the woods and not be disturbed. I'm beginning to think his idea of disturbed was a little warped. There are red and white drapes that hang over the floor-to-ceiling glass walls in the waiting area to the left, which overlooks the woods. The reception is directly in front of the main entrance, and to the right is where the round stairwell leads you to the bedrooms upstairs.

"Come on, Madison," the woman says, and it's then I realize I didn't catch her name. She must see the look that goes across my face, because she smiles, waving her hand in the air. "How rude of me."

I step inside, taking her outstretched hand. "I'm Katsia. Nice to meet you."

And that's when everything stops.

CHAPTER 13

She's still smiling when I tilt my head, looking over to her. She doesn't catch my surprise, or I hide it well because her smile doesn't drop.

What.

The.

Fuck?

Shaking my head, I figured I must have misheard. "Sorry," I answer shyly. "Hi, I'm Madison. Sorry, I didn't quite catch your name?"

"Katsia!" she repeats, none the wiser. I shake her hand and mentally slap myself. I knew I shouldn't have driven off, but if I leave now, will she know that I *know*? Whatever it is that I think I know. It would be too obvious if I did, though. And then she might kill me with her sharp-as-fuck stilettos, and I've had enough near-death experiences to last me a lifetime, so I play dumb.

"Nice to meet you, Katsia."

"Come on." She waves me over, and I follow as she heads toward the front reception desk where two more young men are working. All are wearing the same uniform as the valet, only when these boys look at me—I feel nothing. Nothing like I felt with the boy outside. One is of darker complexion, a stoic look on his face, and the other looks Hispanic. They both straighten their shoulders when they see us walking toward them.

"Miss K." They both do a small bow, and I look toward Katsia again before looking back to the boys who haven't glanced at her but rather kept their eyes straight ahead.

"Thank you. Please, give me Montgomery's key."

I watch as their eyes widen in shock but don't move from their position, locked on the wall ahead.

"Now," Katsia urges, and they jump, spinning around and disappearing behind a small door.

"Excuse me." I clear my throat, figuring this might be a good time to ask. "But can I ask how you know who I am?"

Katsia turns to face me, her eyes staring into mine with an unreadable expression. It's a mix between awe and something else I can't quite peg. "Well, I guess we can chat about that once you're all settled in. I'd like to show you the grounds, if you don't mind. I know you haven't been here since you were a little girl." Deciding I don't want to appear as if I'm onto her or know anything about *The Book*, I nod before going back to waiting for the boys to return with the key. Because, really, I shouldn't be that surprised. My dad could have told me about this place. I can't show an inkling of my knowledge of the Kings, because I don't know this woman or what she's capable of.

The boys return, the darker one handing Katsia the key. "Here you go, ma'am."

She takes it and gestures toward the stairwell. "I'll show you to your room, Madison." We walk up the stairs and down the long, dimly lit hallway, passing red doors with gold numbers attached to them. The hallway is a lot longer than I remembered it to be.

Forget.

Reaching the end, Katsia pushes a button and elevator doors ping open. Stepping inside the small enclosure, the doors close, classical music dancing between the silence. I'm not a fan of this particular genre, but anything beats complete silence when in an enclosed space with someone you're not sure is a good or a shitty person.

The doors slide open and we walk out then down another long hallway, only now the walls are glistening in gold paint, and the doors are all licked in white. It's interesting how vivid the two colors are, but maybe that's part of their deco and what they were aiming for. One would hope. If Tatum sees it, she'll flip out, what with her deco-loving brain. Thinking of Tatum, I need to text her just in case I don't make it through the weekend.

We reach a door, but where there were numbers marking the red doors, on these there seems to be some sort of foreign writing on them. I can't make out the name because the cursive font is hard to read, let alone it being in a completely different language, so I brush it off for now.

Katsia pushes the key into the hole and opens the door. "I can meet you back downstairs when you're all settled and ready."

I nod, taking the key from her and stepping inside. Shutting the door behind me, I walk in, dropping my bag on the floor. The room, if it's the same one I was in as a child, looks unrecognizable. Skimming my hands over the old oak wood that lines the deep gold walls, I check out the rest of the room. A large California king bed is tucked away to the left, on a platform that overlooks the woods from the floor-to-ceiling windows. There's an en suite, walk-in closet, a fully functioning and stocked bar, but no TV.

Walking to the other side of the room, I open up a cabinet, thinking a TV might be hidden in there, only it opens up to a fully loaded cabinet full of guns. Semi-automatics, shotguns, the works. This is not surprising. There was a reason why dad liked bringing me here; it's obviously a free-for-all ranch that supported the second amendment. Closing the cabinet, I pick my bag up and take it to the bed, pulling out all of my clothes. Deciding there's no way I'm going to make an effort with my attire, I shove everything back inside and take out some skinny jeans and a long-sleeve shirt.

Slipping into the shower, I scrub up in double-time—even though I want to sit there forever. I seriously need to talk to Dad about getting a showerhead that fills the entire shower stall, because that shit's amazing. Shuffling into my clothes, I let my hair down and fluff it up to fall in my natural curls, skip the makeup, and shove on my Chucks. I came here to shoot, not to play Clue with Mrs. Robinson, but color me intrigued. Although not much surprises me anymore since meeting the Kings and discovering the history, this has me enthralled enough to sit down and chat.

When I walk into the main lobby, the young valet from earlier is talking to Katsia. From where I'm standing, I can't make out what they're saying, but judging by the movements of his hands and the expressions on his face, they're not talking about anything light.

The boy—who I should probably stop calling "boy"—stops his talking, his mouth slamming shut before he inches his head toward me slightly, like he felt me enter the room. Well, the connection is mutual, and I have no idea what to make of it at all. His eyes lock onto mine and something pangs in my chest. Recognition, guilt, confusion. They all swim inside me, and I have no idea what to do with it. He storms away from Katsia and into the back of the reception area. Katsia continues watching him with careful eyes. She looks back to me, plastering on a, what seems like, a fake smile before waving me over.

I walk toward her. "Sorry, didn't mean to interrupt."

She brushes my words off casually. "Don't you worry about Damon. You hungry?" she asks, leading me into the large restaurant on the other side of the stairwell. I remember this place a little, but walking into it, it's like I've never been here before. Everything has changed and been upgraded. Chandeliers hang from the high ceilings, and all-glass walls line the entire room so you have a vast view of the woods anywhere you sit. We take a table on the other side of the room, tucked away enough for privacy.

She picks up the menu and smiles. "The fish is good. If you still like fish, that is."

Smiling, but not sure of the angle she's aiming for, I nod. "Love fish."

The waiter comes and takes our menus, and as she suspected, I ordered the salmon and steamed veggies. Pouring us both a glass of water, she looks at me. "So, how'd I know who you were?" she asks my unspoken question with a smile.

Nodding, I take a sip of water.

"Well, I've known your father for a while now."

"I sort of figured that. I remember this place a little," I answer, placing my glass down.

"How much do you remember?" She aims for casual, but I pick up the hitch in her tone, and though the question could be interpreted as one that has a double meaning, she says it with such etiquette that it doesn't have me second-guessing her intention. In fact, if I hadn't read some of *The Book*, and if I didn't know what I knew about my father and the Kings, her question and the way she said it would've slipped right past me.

"Not that much. I just remember him bringing me here as a kid. He would say it was his freedom. I just needed to get grounded a bit more."

"Oh?" That perks her attention. I once again caught her tone. As if she realizes she may have seemed a little too interested, she drops her smile a notch. "Well, I hope we can give that to you." The waiter comes, placing breadsticks and garlic bread on the center of the table, and I reach for one immediately, wanting something to occupy myself with that doesn't include being interrogated.

"Yeah." I shrug like any other teenager would. "I mean, just school and my friends. It's all a little much. My love for shooting only intensified as I got older, and I don't know," I mutter. "I guess I wanted a change of scenery and to get away for a bit."

She nods as if in understanding, but I can see a thousand questions hidden behind that calm and collected posture she's holding so well. "How long do you plan on staying?"

"Just the night. I have school on Monday, so I should get back tomorrow afternoon sometime."

She smiles in acknowledgment. "Well, I hope you enjoy your stay." The waiter comes back, placing both our dishes on the table and leaving. Picking up a fork, I slice into the salmon and place some in my mouth, it melting in an instant. Fighting the urge to moan in approval, I chew slowly while picking up my water.

"So you and my dad are good friends still?"

She pauses her chewing and swallows. "Well of course. I assume he told you to come here?"

"Actually, he doesn't know where I am right now. I just packed my car and left. I remembered this place and drove." She places her knife and fork down, dabbing the napkin over her mouth.

"So he doesn't know you're here?" she clarifies, though I already said that.

"He doesn't, no. Is that a problem?" Tilting my head, I watch her reaction.

Her face relaxes before she smiles. "No. No problem."

The bitch is good. Whatever she's playing at, she's good at it. Getting to her feet, she smiles, but not enough for it to reach her eyes. "Make yourself at home, Madison," she murmurs in a way that has chills breaking out down my spine. "I'm sure there's enough here to keep you occupied with your time." Then she leaves in a hurry.

Turning back to my food, I toss the salmon around on my plate, thinking over what the fuck just happened. Who is this woman and why is her name Katsia? Deciding the salmon is way too good to go to waste, I finish it all before washing it down with my water. Leaning into my chair, I think over my options—which, admittedly, isn't much. I could text Nate, or Bishop, and ask them about this new finding. But that would defeat my purpose of getting away, because I know they'll both be here in a flash to get me. Then again, they might be able to give me answers, ones I so desperately need because of this new discovery.

Exhaling, I pick up my glass and take a sip. No, I can't do that. For one, I have too much pride, and two… I have too much pride. I'll just have to figure this shit out on my own and hope I don't get killed in the process. Swallowing the cool water, movement catches my eye from the outside patio, and I look toward it. Noticing the outline of the valet's hat, I get to my feet, drop a couple of bills, and head toward the doors, which are open, displaying the cool woodsy night. There are tea lights outlining the wooden rails that frame the porch and a couple of rocking chairs that sit looking out toward the forest. Looking from left to right, I catch the boy's back as he turns and disappears around a corner. Gaining a bit of speed in my walk, I follow him. Just as I turn the corner, a hand comes to my mouth.

"Shhh," a voice whispers into my ear before I have a chance to scream bloody murder. "I—I not hurt you. Nod if I let go and you no scream."

I nod, feeling like I've dodged being killed enough times to be able to write a book about not getting killed. He releases and I spin around, my breath catching as I attempt to slow my erratic heartbeat.

"What the fuck?" I whisper-yell toward him. "Was that necessary?"

His response is instant. "Yes."

My mouth snaps closed as I study him closer. Close up,

he looks a little older than me, now that I can see some imperfections on his face, but still young. His eyes are a warm chocolate brown, circled with long eyelashes.

"Who are you?" I ask, not fully comprehending what I should be asking, but I figured asking who he is was a good start, and it gives me a few seconds to gain my wits after his surprise.

"Damon. You're Madison Montgomery?"

"Damon?" I whisper, searching his face for clues.

"Yes," he responds through his broken English, "It's Latin. You are Madison?"

"No, I just like to pretend to be her, you know, because the perks are *awesome*." I can't help the sarcasm. His face remains poised, still, and unimpressed with my sense of humor. He's a little serious and a lot dry. "It's a joke," I deadpan after the silence gets awkward.

"A joke?" He tests out the word on his tongue. "What is joke mean?"

Tilting my head, I narrow my eyes. "What do you mean?" Something seems off about this kid, and it has fear creeping into my throat.

"*Non fueris locutus sum valde bonum…*," he begins, and I suck in a breath in confusion. He notices my puzzlement and then corrects himself. "Sorry, I mean, I don't fluent English." Well, that makes a whole lot of sense, and makes this thing a lot more complicated.

"Okay," I answer slowly. "What is your language?" Maybe it's Spanish. My God, I hope it's Spanish, because I know a lot of that.

"Latin."

Fuck.

Rubbing my forehead, I shake my head. "I know jack shit about Latin. Okay." I look up to him, his face still the same, like a lost puppy bursting at the seams to speak but only knowing how to bark. I can almost feel the frustration radiating off of him.

"You," I point to him, "meet me in my room in fifteen minutes. It's not safe here."

He nods. "Number?"

"No, I'm on the Gold Level. I don't know what the name says on my door, but I'll put this…" I pull out a piece of paper from my pocket. "…on my door. Okay? Understand?"

He seems to think over my words and then nods. "Yes, I understand."

Jesus fucking Christ. Of course my only way of finding something out here only speaks fucking Latin.

There's that language again.

Nodding, I set off on my quest back to my room, slowly coming to the realization I may not be getting as much shooting done as I had initially hoped.

Pacing back and forth in my room, I wait as the time passes. It's been forty minutes since I told him to meet me back here, and I'm starting to get impatient. My phone ringing has merely settled into background music until I finally give up.

"Oh for fuck's sake!" Walking to the bedside table, I pick up my phone, sliding it open and bringing it to my ear. "What?"

"Don't fucking *what* me, Madison. Where the fuck are

you?" Bishop growls down the phone.

"I'm away. I'll be back tomorrow night."

"That didn't answer my question."

"Well good thing I don't have to answer to any of your questions!" There's a knock on the door, a slight tap I could have missed had it been two seconds earlier with Bishop growling in my ear. Changing hands, I walk toward the door and pull it open, seeing Damon on the other side.

"I gotta go," I mumble into the phone.

"Sorry I'm late," Damon mutters, walking past me and into my room.

"Who the fuck is that?" Bishop shoots off in my ear.

"That is… I can't explain right now, so just wait until I get home."

"I swear to fucking—"

I hang up my phone and switch it off, having about enough of his bullshit. Turning around, I smile at Damon. "Sorry about that."

He sits on the chair across from my bed, his back straight and his hands placed rigidly on his thighs. His face stays the same, his eyes remaining on me as I slowly make my way to sit on the end of my bed. "So," I test out, not knowing what else to start with. "How are we going to do this if your language is Latin?" I ask myself the question more than him.

"You are in danger here. You must leave."

Well, that's a pretty good way to start. "I figured," I whisper, bringing my eyes back to his. "But why? And why are you helping me?"

He shakes his head, his eyes glassing over. "Knowledge not power. Knowledge in this world can be a weapon, or a reason." He stands from his chair and walks toward me, stopping just at the foot of the bed. A little close, but I don't feel uncomfortable about it. He takes my hand and I freeze slightly, unfamiliar with his presence, but again, not uncomfortable with it.

Pressing my hand to his chest, I look up at him, my heart pounding in my chest. "What is this?" I ask, shaking my head.

"You feel too?" he replies, so softly it almost takes my breath away. Being with emotionless assholes for way too long has me appreciating a man who has no problem with displaying his feelings. If that's what he's doing.

"Yes." Unable to lie, or deny it, and not wanting to, I stand to all my five foot three inches and crank my neck so I can see him more clearly. "Who are you?"

"I'm not good man."

I laugh. I don't mean to, but I do. "I know bad men, Damon. You are not one of them."

"Only you see light where others see dark, Madison."

Shaking my head, I pull my hand away. "Maybe. But I see dark too, Damon. And I don't see it on you."

"Because it's caged in my soul," he replies, taking a step back.

"Who are you?" I whisper again, searching his beautiful features. The angelic way he carries himself and the way he looks straight into me tells me he's deluded. He's not a bad man; there's no way this person standing in front of me right now is bad.

He sits back down, burying his face in his hands and shaking his head. "You..." he begins. "The Silver Swan."

I gulp, my blood turning slightly cold. "Yes."

He whips his head up to me and narrows his eyes slightly. Probably the most display of emotion I've seen on him as far as features go. "You… know? About yourself?" he asks again, his English choppy but enough for me to understand what he's trying to say or imply.

I nod. "Yes. I've known for some time now."

His face changes. "You must leave, Madison."

"No." I shake my head. "I'm stubborn. I have to know what this all means. I came here for clarity, to get my feet back on the ground, but I have a feeling that isn't happening now." I look at him as he watches me. I realize he probably has no idea what I just said, but I appreciate him listening anyway.

He gets up from his chair and walks toward the door. As he pulls it open, I think he's about to walk out when he widens it, checking down the hallway, but he looks back to me. "See?" He points to the cursive name on the door.

I look to it and nod. "Yeah? I don't know what that says."

He runs his index finger over the embossed lettering, every flick and curve that is inscribed into the door. He says one word. One word that sucks all the good out of my thoughts and replaces it with murky memories. "Venari."

CHAPTER 14

I SHOOT UP OFF THE BED AND WALK TOWARD HIM, pulling him back inside the room before slamming the door, resting my head against it. "How the fuck do you know that name?"

He shakes his head. "I know"—his arms widen—"everything, Madison."

Locking my eyes on his, I nod. "Okay, it's settled." Pushing off the door, I go straight to my bag and start shoving all my belongings back inside. "You're coming home with me."

"No!" he answers, walking toward me and halting my arm. Not roughly, but enough for me to realize this boy is a lot stronger than what he looks.

Interesting.

"I can't leave," he continues, releasing my arm.

"Why not?" I zip up my bag anyway.

"Katsia... she...."

"Who the fuck is she?" I drop my tone an inch. "Seriously, Damon, I've read the title-less book. Her diary or suicide note or whatever!"

Damon's eyes turn hard and cold. "*Tacet a Mortuis.*"

"Pardon?" I ask, confused with his Latin again.

"*Tacet a Mortuis* is the name of the book. In English is *Whispers from the Dead.*"

"Oh." My eyebrows pull together in confusion. *The Book* is still easier to say than *Tacet a Mortuis*, but okay.

A look flashes over his face. "Where is that book?"

"Um, it's at my house. Why?" Dammit. I shouldn't be so quick with trusting people.

"You must take care of it. People—" He stops. "I must leave now."

"No!" I yell to his retreating back. "Please, you're my only hope in figuring out what the fuck this world all means!"

"I've said too much. I will be punished. I'm sorry, Madison." Then he walks out the door, the silence of his departure deafening.

Huffing out a breath, I sit on my bed.

What did he mean he would be punished? None of this makes fucking sense. Everything that should be simple is a fucking vortex of mind-fuckery, and the only person I can really rely on is myself. Deciding I won't be getting any sleep tonight, I pick up my packed bag and walk toward the door. If I need to escape quickly, I don't want to have to leave anything behind. Running down the hallway, I reach the elevator and press the down arrow a few hundred times before it dings open. Thanking my lucky stars it's empty, I walk in and press on the Ground key. Once I reach the lobby, I step out and look around, scanning the area to make sure Katsia isn't walking around before dashing out the front sliding doors, narrowly dodging the two reception boys at the desk. Why are they working throughout the night? I doubt anyone else would be checking in at this time.

The cold air hits me like a breath of fresh air when I see Damon. Quickly, I walk toward him. "Hey." I look over my shoulder out of paranoia.

"Madison, what are you doing?" He looks around, making sure no one is behind me.

"Look, I just need to put these into my car in case I need to get out of here fast."

Damon watches me closely before nodding and pulling my arm so I follow him to his valet desk. He unhooks my keys and hands them to me. "Parking spot fifteen. Madison, you must leave now."

I shake my head. "No. I need answers. I'm sick of waiting for people to tell me when they're ready. I need to know now."

"I can't." He shakes his head. "Madison. I have person very close to me who will be in danger if I tell anything."

I smile. "It's okay, Damon. I can figure it all out on my own."

"No." He shakes his head. "You not understand."

"I do," I reply softly, touching his arm. "I understand. I have people who I'd protect too."

He shakes his head again. "Person is you, Madison."
Wait.

I squeeze the keys in my hand. "Me?"

He nods. "Etiam."

"But you only just met me."

His eyes glare into mine, the stare so strong I almost

flinch at the electricity that passes between us. "You think this first time we've met?"

A long stretch of silence passes through us as I look from one eye to the other. "I… I—" But even as I'm about to say it, I know I do remember. "I—yes? I don't know, Damon!" Feeling myself getting frustrated at all the mystery, I blow out a whoosh of air. "Tell me."

He grips my arm again and starts tugging me toward the parking lot. "Come."

I follow, noticing how his grip loosens as we get closer to my car, like he knows I'm safer the closer I get. "Open." He gestures toward the SUV, and I obey, beeping it unlocked as we both slip inside. I toss my bag to the back and shut my door, the enclosed space feeling safer to talk now.

"You gotta give me something here, Damon. What is Venari? What does that mean? I haven't heard that word since—"

"Lucan," he finishes for me, and I flinch, my heart crushing in my chest at someone else saying that name.

"How?" I ask, fighting the tears, fighting the memories. I feel the dark murky fog rising inside of me, slowly seeping into my inner peace, and threatening to shatter every single thing I worked hard for over the years.

Damon looks at me. "I'm Lost Boy."

"A what?" That had nothing to do with what I asked, but I know his English isn't very good, so I go with it.

"Lost Boy. How much book have you seen?" he asks, the words jumbled, but again, I understand what he's trying to ask.

"I'm up to 11 I think."

His jaw tenses. "You have far to go."

"Like, how far?" I know how thick the book is, but I was sort of hoping it wasn't that long.

"Final page 66/6."

"Well, that's poetic. The mark of the beast, just great."

Damon looks to me, his features frozen. "Sixty-six chapters, six pages in final."

"Did she mean to do that?" I ask.

"No," he shakes his head, "she not. You learn about Lost Boys soon. I am them."

"Okay." I look around the car. "But how do you know so much about me?"

"I just do. We all do. But I know the most."

"Why?" I ask, needing to know more information. "Why do you know the most? Why do I feel a connection to you I've never felt before? Why is it that I trust you even though I trust barely anyone?"

He looks at me. "You are my sister. I'm your twin."

CHAPTER 15

"**W**HAT THE FUCK?" I SHOOT UP IN MY CHAIR, hitting my head on the top of the ceiling. "No... no, that makes no sense at all, because my mom and dad would have told me. And that makes no sense because that would mean you would be a King, but you're not. You're a lost boy, and you're here, living this..." I look outside. "...weird-as-fuck life, and my mom and dad are actually good people. I mean, I'd like to think they're good people and they would never leave you to be living this life and—*what the fuck*?" I repeat after my freak out. "Okay."

Breath in and out. Slow intakes of breath.

One.

Two.

Three.

I look at him, but his face is still the same. He's watching me in fascination, like I'm a foreign object he wants to learn about. "Don't do that," I murmur, suddenly realizing how uncomfortable it's making me now, because it's as though he can read my thoughts.

"I can." He nods.

"What?" I snap. I swear to God, if this turns all supernatural-y, I will demand that Dean Winchester roar into my life in his fucking muscle car and sweep me off my feet, or I'm done.

"I read what you think, but not because I read mind. Because I read your expressions. You need to control them."

"My expressions are fine the way they are."

"Fine?" he asks, confused with the word.

Oh, sweet mother of God. I came here to relax, and instead, I've been thrown into a pool of more questions. Finally calming my breathing enough to ponder his revelation, I turn in my seat. "If that's true, and you are my brother, my twin brother—"

"It's true. I do not lie, Madison."

"Let me finish." The way he cuts into my conversation has me thinking he's obviously my brother.

"Why? Why are you here? Why did Mom and Dad not tell me about you?"

"Those are questions I not answer. Not me. Not now. Another time. You must go."

"No!" I yell, just as his hand touches the door handle. "You can't drop a bomb like that and leave! What is this place?" I look up to the ranch and then back to him. His eyes are sad as he looks back to me.

"Hell."

"Who else lives here?" I ask, pressing with more questions

and wanting him to bleed out more answers.

"Katsia and Lost Boys."

"Katsia is your boss?"

He shakes his head. "Katsia owns Lost Boys."

He goes to open the door again, and I stop him. "What? This is obviously not the same Katsia as the one in the book." Again, I remind myself about my earlier statement of Dean Winchester.

He looks back at me, confused. "Never mind. But is she good or is she bad?" Though I already know the answer to this, I just need clarification. I've been wrong in the past.

"*Malus*," he whispers, finally getting out of the car. I inch up off my seat, reaching for my phone in my back pocket, and switch it on. *Malus*? This fucking language is going to kill me one day. Typing *Malus* into google translate, the word *Bad* comes up in the little white box. Great, as suspected, she's bad. Are there any good people left in this world?

Leaning back in my chair, I think over what my options are right now. I could leave, tell the boys, and then come back and get Damon. But what if they already know I have a brother? What if they already know about this place? About Katsia? No, I've only got myself. Tilting my head, I look toward the ranch again, watching as Damon stands outside the main entrance, his hands behind his back and his eyes remaining forward. Such posture, poise, and discipline.

Starting the car, I put it into Drive and head toward the front entrance, where Damon is standing. He looks at my truck and then quickly looks behind him, checking to make sure no one is coming. Pulling open the passenger door, his jaw tenses. "What are you doing, Madison?"

"Get in."

"I can't—"

"Get the fuck in this car now, Damon. I'm dead serious. Nothing will happen to you." He looks over his shoulder and then looks back to me. Removing his hat, he tosses it across the sidewalk and gets into the passenger seat, slamming the door behind him. Skidding out of the ranch, I make my way down the long driveway, the darkness of the night soaking through all the trees. During the day, this driveway looks incredible, all bright colors and positive energy, but at night, it looks like it could be the driveway to Hades. The trees reach over the long road, casting shadows in the night. I look toward Damon, the dash lights illuminating his features a smidge.

"Are you okay?"

He shakes his head. "This is not good. Katsia—"

"Will do nothing," I snap, then relax a little. "Look, I don't know if you can understand fully what I'm saying, but I'm going to go with it anyway. I don't know who I can trust in this world or who I can't. I've trusted the wrong people before, and it won't be the last time, but I trust you."

He looks to me now, his eyes softening. "You trust me?"

"Yes," I respond, taking my eyes back to the road ahead and making a right turn onto the main highway. "I can't explain how or why, but I do. But know this," I murmur. "I won't let anything happen to you, Damon."

"I don't need your protection, Madison."

"I know. But Katsia won't do anything."

"You not understand," he whispers. "I'm the alpha Lost Boy." Even the word alpha sounds weird coming out of his mouth because he doesn't seem like that kind of guy to me. I haven't seen him in an alpha form, so I giggle a little.

"Madison," he shakes his head in disdain, "so much you don't know."

"Well, we have a forty-minute drive back."

"You never should come back, Madison."

I look at him then the road and then back to him. "What? Why?"

"He knew no take you there but did anyway."

"Who?"

He looks at me dead in the eye. "*Your* father."

The drive back was done in silence after Damon's little outburst of how I shouldn't be back in the Hamptons. I wanted to press to learn why, but I can't. Not yet. I can see how Damon will only share what he wants to share, and he's not the type of person that can be swayed.

We pull into our underground garage, and I look at the clock in the dash. Just past midnight, so everyone should be asleep, if my dad and Elena are even home. I don't see Nate's car anywhere, so I know he's not in for the night. Probably out terrorizing some poor girl. Pushing the button to close the garage door, I get out of the car and round to the passenger side. Damon follows, shutting the door behind him.

"Come on. You can sleep in my room until I figure some stuff out."

"I can't stay." He shakes his head.

"The fuck you can't." I take his arm, and he tenses at my touch, yanking away from me.

"Sorry," he mutters when he sees the shock on my face.

"It's okay. So you don't like being touched. That's probably the least of the weird thing I've come across as far as phobias go." Beeping the car, I make my way toward the door with Damon following closely behind me.

"It's not a phobia," he confesses, just as we make our way up the stairs to the main living area.

I turn over my shoulder a little. "It's okay. You don't have to talk about it."

He pauses, his eyes searching my face before he nods. "Thank you."

I smile softly, and then round the stairs, taking the first step. "I'll get some of Nate's clothes for you. He won't mind, and even if he did, he could eat a fat...." I notice he's not following me anymore and turn around, finding him still on the first step and looking to the ground like he's trying to add something up in his head. "Damon?"

"Nate?" he whispers. "Nate?" he repeats, searching the ground once more.

"Yes?" I take a tentative step back down. "Nate Riverside?"

Damon stills. "Not Riverside."

Huh? I swear this is too much. "We can finish all these conversations tomorrow. Come on, let's get some sleep." I reach my hand out to him and he takes it, letting me lead him up the stairs and into my room. As soon as he's inside, he pauses, looking around.

"No pink?"

I shake my head. "Not a pink girl."

Damon looks like he wants to giggle, but doesn't. In fact, I don't recall ever seeing him smile, much less giggle. "Not surprising."

I tilt my head. "I'll set you up on the floor. I'll just go and get something for you to wear from Nate's room." Though Nate is noticeably larger than Damon, I'm pretty sure he can make it work until I take him to get new clothes.

Slipping into my bathroom, I open Nate's door, the dark room a little creepy. Hitting the light, I walk straight to Nate's closet.

"The fuck are you doing, sis?"

"Shit!" I scream, spinning around and coming face-to-face with Nate. Damon comes barging through the door, his eyes feral and his stance stiff. "It's okay!" I tell Damon, noticing how he looks about ready to rip someone's head off.

He isn't looking like the Damon I've just met and spent a bit of time with.

"And who the fuck are you?" Nate quips, getting out of bed with his Calvin Klein briefs on.

"Nate, get back into bed."

"No," he says, narrowing his eyes on Damon. "I *know* you."

"No, you don't," I brush him off while praying he doesn't so I can leave this conversation until tomorrow. I'm hungry, tired, and I didn't get the rest I wanted and needed, so I'm about ready to jump off the cliff of "calm and collected" and dive straight into the ocean of "lost my shit" with five-foot swells of "I'll kill you all."

"Yes," Nate continues, slowly stepping closer and closer to Damon. "You…" Something clicks in his head, and he suddenly launches toward Damon, his fist flying toward his face.

"Nate!" I scream, throwing myself toward the two of them, but latching onto Nate's back, my arms connecting around his throat. Damon swerves, dodging his punch calmly, his face not showing any distress. He looks almost disinterested—bored.

Nate falls to the ground with me on top of him.

"What the fuck?" I slap Nate on the back. "Dick!"

Nate flips me on my ass and gets to his feet, pointing down at me. "Stay the fuck there." Then he turns to Damon. "*I fucking know you.*"

I get to my feet. "Leave him alone."

Damon looks to Nate. "I know you do."

"Shut up, Damon!" I snap. He needs to shut his mouth before he says something stupid. Hopefully, he'll say it in Latin.

Nate tilts his head. "*Et tu puer vetustus amissus….*"

Well, there goes that theory.

"You speak fucking Latin?" I yell toward Nate, but he throws his hand up, halting me. Getting my phone out of my pocket, I quickly pull up the translate app, so I can type at least one word I catch into the program. I snap my mouth closed, sensing the tense energy in the room. It's almost like two devils have come head-to-head, and one of them is going down. It's eerie, creepy, and goose bumps break out over my spine at just how seriously terrifying this is.

Damon's stance changes. The air shifts as his shoulders square, his eyes break into black marbles, and his lip curls.

I step back, realizing how little I know about him. His entire being just morphed in front of my very eyes. No longer is he the quiet valet boy who speaks hardly any English. Now, I'm seeing him—as he put it—the Alpha Lost boy.

"*Pueri et im amissa.*"

Lost Boy.

Okay, so Nate knows about them. Or something was said about the Lost Boys. Of fucking course he does.

"Well this is all great and everything, but I'm tired—"

"Madison! Shut up!" Nate snaps at me.

He turns back toward Damon, stepping closer. My

fingers twitch, wanting to get between them to stop any other altercation from happening. "*Non potes habere eam*," Nate seethes, his lip curled and his steps calculated. Like a hungry tiger, waiting to take its kill on his prey.

Can't have her.

Okay, what the fuck?

"Have me?" I ask, looking up from my phone. "What are you two actually fuckin—"

The door bangs open, revealing Bishop standing there, his dark hoodie over his head, in his loose, torn jeans, and with his combat boots on his feet. His eyes scan over me first before going to Nate and Damon.

"Are you kidding me?" I yell, quickly making my way toward Damon.

Nate is lethal; he could snap someone's neck with his bare hands and not blink, but Bishop? Bishop is a different level entirely. He'd not only snap your neck; he'd dissect your body piece-by-piece and send each of your organs to a member of your family.

"Madison," Bishop growls. It's so low, it catches my breath. I look toward him, but press my back against Damon. Bishop's eyes are dark, almost black, his head down slightly, his jaw tense, and his lip curled in disgust. He doesn't flinch. All his focus is solely on Damon. "Get the fuck out of my way."

"No!" I snap. "Damon isn't like the others, whatever they're like. I wouldn't know, because I don't speak motherfucking Latin!" I'm losing my shit a bit, but I'm sick of being the quiet voice in the house.

"Madison. Get the fuck out of the way before I fucking move you myself."

"Madison," Damon says gently from behind me, and I shiver at the cool calmness of his voice. It's petrifying, but peaceful. I know he won't hurt me, so I trust him.

"Shh," I hush him over my shoulder before looking back to both Nate and Bishop.

"Now both of you are going to let me finish speaking." I look between the two of them. "Damon left Katsia—and yes, I know about Katsia, and before you both fly off the handle, I drove to the ranch, not knowing what it was, only remembering what is was like there as a kid."

Forget.

I take a big gulp of air. "I needed a fucking break from you guys, so I drove to the only place I remember my dad taking me as a kid—that ranch. It wasn't until I got there and met Damon and then Katsia..." I shake my head, still in shock from that revelation. "...that I realized the place was something else entirely. I look toward Bishop, his eyes still on Damon like he's ready to feast on him for dessert.

"Bishop?" I narrow my eyes. "Did you guys know he's my brother? My twin?"

Bishop's focus snaps straight to me before going back to Damon. "*Et nuntiatum est illi?*"

"Stop fucking talking in Latin!" I yell, annoyed with everyone even though the way the syllables roll off Bishop's tongue has my lady bits tingling. "Did you both know?" I repeat, looking toward Bishop and Nate.

"Yes," Bishop answers, dropping his hoodie to sit around his neck. He cranks his shoulders, rolling them out before looking back to Damon. "But that doesn't mean shit. You shouldn't trust him."

"Why?" I scoff. "Like I shouldn't have trusted you?"

His mouth snaps closed. "That's different."

I roll my eyes and look back to Damon. "Go into my room. I'm okay. I'll handle it."

Damon pauses then nods. "Okay." He turns and walks back to my room, and I shut Nate's door, spinning around to look at both boys. "The fuck is your problem?"

"Madison," Nate says, his tone empty of any humor. This is Nate's serious voice, and usually I take it seriously, but they need to trust *me* now.

"No, Nate. I trust him. He's not going to hurt me."

Nate steps toward me, but Bishop's hand comes up to his shoulder, stopping him. He looks toward Bishop, and Bishop shakes his head. "I'll handle this."

I swallow.

Bishop walks toward me, his finger hooking under my chin to nudge my head up. He looks down, towering over me. "First thing I'm going to say is that when I say you don't trust someone, Madison, I usually mean you don't *fucking* trust someone. Second thing? Do you know what the Lost Boys' job is, Madison? What their *main* job is? What Katsia is? Who she is?" His fingers spread over my cheeks as he push-es me backward until I hit the wall behind me. He drops his tone, his hand squeezing my cheeks so tightly my lips pucker. "I'm so fucking angry at you, Kitty. I don't know whether I should *fuck* you or *kill* you or *both*," he whispers angrily, his lip curled and his breath falling over mine. My heart pounds in my chest.

Oh, God. I've really pissed him off. Usually, I enjoy this, but not when I see the anger lingering in his eyes. That anger is a caged beast, seconds away from breaking free.

"Of course I don't know, Bishop." I nudge my head, trying

to get my face out of his grip, but he doesn't budge. Instead, he steps in between my legs and pins my waist to the wall with his, feeling his cock push into my stomach.

Narrowing my eyes, I look down to his perfect lips. "You don't tell me shit."

His jaw tenses, and then a smirk licks the corner of his mouth. But it's not a nice smirk. This is Bishop's other smirk. The one I saw when he slit Ally's throat. Fear whistles through my bones, just lightly. Enough to make me brace myself for what's to come.

He brings his mouth to my ear. "When I fucking say don't trust someone, Madison. You don't trust them."

"What do they do?" I ask, closing my eyes.

Please don't say what I think you're going to say.

"Lost Boys?" Nate grins, walking up behind Bishop. "Who do you think takes care of the little Swans, Madison?"

"Take care?" My eyebrows furrow. I look to Nate, his grin not changing. My stomach curls in disgust as realization sinks into my thought process. "Oh my God."

Bishop's hand moves from my face to my throat, and he squeezes slowly. "Gotta say, this is getting my dick hard like nothing. It's a dangerous thing you have me feeling, Kitty. The angrier you make me, the more I want to fuck you until you're so fucking bruised that you feel the wrath of my anger for weeks after."

"But... but he won't hurt me." I ignore his sick innuendo.

"Oh?" Nate scoffs, walking to the little bar fridge he has in the corner of his room, pulling out a bottled water. He looks to me in disbelief. "What? Because you're fucking blood? That doesn't mean shit, Madison. He's not a good person. He is probably here to obtain you—ever think of that?"

Nate tosses the bottle onto his bed and walks back toward Bishop—who hasn't released my throat—and me.

"What about Katsia?" I ask. "Who the fuck is she and what does she play in this game? She's obviously the descendant of the Katsia in *The Book*—sorry," I correct myself, "*Tacet de Mortues*." In a flash, Bishop squeezes tight and slams me up against the wall again. "Who the fuck told you that?"

"What?" I wheeze out. "Let go, Bishop!"

He loosens his grip, but when I look into his eyes, I see it. That same caged beast. This is the other side to Bishop I'm talking with right now, and I'm not sure I like it anymore.

"Bro." Nate notices Bishop's shift. "Step back."

"Fuck off, Nate."

Nate looks to me and then to Bishop, knowing he can't say anything. Bishop loosens his grip and I nod at Nate, signaling he's released it.

I stretch my neck. "Do that again, and I'll knee you in the nuts, grab my .45, and shoot your fucking hand clean off."

Bishop smirks, his tongue running over his bottom lip. "You do that..." His eyes dance in mischief—black magic kind of mischief. "...and I'll wash your hair with my blood while you choke on my dick."

"More like I'll bite it off," I mutter, challenging the devil himself.

"Naw, baby. You and I both know you love it too much."

"Fuck you. I'll cut it off and make you watch as I fuck—"

"As excited as I am about this very disturbing and very sick dirty talk—" Nate looks between Bishop and me. "—seriously, y'all need help—we have a *very* serious matter that is currently sitting in the next room."

I shove Bishop, and he steps up to me again in challenge,

his chest brushing against mine, bringing my nipples to life. Fuck. Why do both our hormones have to feed on hate? I'm fucked.

I bring my palm to Bishop's chest, narrowing my eyes at him. "Anyway." I look toward Nate. "Okay, so what does Katsia play in this? In the book, she was good."

"*She*, being the original, yes," Nate murmurs, taking a seat on the end of his bed. "But this one… no."

"Who is she? This one, I mean."

"In short," Bishop says, finally getting out of my bubble and grabbing the water bottle Nate tossed onto the bed. "She's—realistically speaking—on our side. She's not a part of The Kings, but Katsia's family have played this role for generations. The one in the book, she started the original Lost Boys."

"The original Lost Boys? But wouldn't that mean she agreed to get rid of the Silver Swans?" I ask, confused. "That makes no sense, because she was always… not like that."

"No," Nate interferes. "That wasn't the original purpose for the Lost Boys."

"What was?" I ask them both.

"How far are you into the book?" Nate asks, looking up at me from under hooded eyes.

"11. Why can't you guys just tell me? Fuck."

"No," Bishop shakes his head, "it's important you read it. We all had to."

"What?" I scoff, sliding down the wall and taking a seat on the hard floor. "You guys all read it?"

They both nod. "After initiation, that was what we had to do."

"That's fucked up," I whisper, looking off into the

distance. "When did my life get so messed up? It's always been messed up, but the more I discover about it, the more questions I have." I look back to both of them. "Will this ever be over?"

They look back at me. "No."

"Well, thanks," I mutter dryly. "Can we just… give Damon a chance? What if he really is on my side, huh? And you guys knock him off when he really could have been helpful!"

"Not taking the chance," Bishop says instantly.

"I wasn't asking you, so sh—"

"Watch your fucking mouth. Everything that has to do with the Kings, Madison, goes through me. Everything to do with you also happens to go through me. So whether you like it or not, *you* go through me. So you may as well do it on your hands and knees with your ass in the air like a good little kitty," he hisses through a smug grin.

"The kitty has claws, so I'd watch it," Nate warns.

Having about enough of Bishop's smartass mouth, I tilt my head. "I don't remember her scratching last night." I smirk at Nate, and he looks back to me, his eyes wide, slowly shaking his head. He brings his hand up to his throat, making a cutting motion for me to stop. Too late, I've committed. Swinging my eyes back to Bishop, his jaw now clenched. "Oh no,"—it's my turn to smirk now—"if I remember correctly…" I pretend to look up to the ceiling, thinking about what I'm going to say next. "…there was a shower… a towel…. Wait!" I throw my hand up and chuckle. "No," I laugh forcefully, looking back to Bishop, my grin wide and my mouth slightly open. "That's right. There was no towel. Just a whole lot of… grinding… kissing… and—"

"Now, bruh, I can explain." Nate quickly gets to his feet, stepping backward with his hands up. "That was not how...." Nate looks to me, his stare evil. "Why you have to open your fucking mouth?" he grounds through gritted teeth.

I smirk.

Nate looks back to Bishop, who is looking directly at Nate with so much hate it makes what he was giving Damon seem like child's play.

Rolling my eyes, because I actually love Nate and don't want to plan his funeral—just yet—I interrupt. "Calm down, Bishop. It was a hard night, and you can't say shit."

"Oh really?" Bishop looks to me. "Because I don't remember the last time I was sucking face with another girl since you, Mads, so fill me in here. Is that what I need to do? Start fucking around so you fucking get where I'm coming from?"

"Bishop," I stand to my feet, "you're being ridiculous. We're not together. Never have been! You're the one who said all that 'no labels' bullshit at the lake."

"Didn't know I had to outline 'don't be a slut,' Madison."

"I'm not a fucking slut!" I yell. "I haven't slept with anyone but you, so fuck you!"

Bishop shakes his head. "Nah, you just like making guys think they can fuck you."

"Fuck—"

"Enough." Damon walks in, shoving his hands into his pockets, still wearing the pants he wore earlier, which reminds me why I'm actually in this room. I turn back to the closet and flick the light on, pulling Nate's clothes out and tossing them over my shoulder.

"What are you doing?" Nate asks, coming toward me. I

fight down the tears that threaten to surface. Truthfully, I had no idea Bishop thought of me in that way. I knew he cared, but not so much that he's willing to use it as a weapon during an argument. My heart feels like it's been shanked with a blunt steak knife and then ripped up to my throat.

Swallowing my emotions, I swipe the stray tears that fell off my cheeks. Fucker made me cry, but I probably asked for it. When you fall for the devil, make sure you don't land face-down with his horns stabbed through your heart. "I'm getting something for Damon to wear."

I feel Nate crouch down beside me, leaning over my shoulder. "Hey—"

"Leave me alone," I whisper, grabbing some sweatpants and a plain white shirt. Admittedly, Nate doesn't have much else aside from assorted ripped jeans and tees.

"No, fuck that. What's wrong? Bishop?" he whispers.

"Everything, Nate. None of this shit makes any sense to me. I feel like I'm slowly losing my mind."

Nate chuckles, and I don't know how, but it takes a little dark smoke out of my feels. "We've all lost our mind, baby, but that's how we all found each other. We're all lost, but we're all lost on the same road."

I look to him; Nate actually making sense. I giggle, sniffling. "There are not a lot of times you've made a hell of a lot of sense, Riverside. But you did just then."

"We're pirates, baby. It's what we do. Now get your bad self up, take whatever you want, but make sure that fucker doesn't ruin any of my clo—For the record," he interrupts himself, "I still don't trust him. But I'm going to trust you, on one condition."

I nod, gripping onto the clothing and internally thanking

whoever is listening that he has agreed. I mean, I would have done it anyway, but having Nate agree just means I get to go make something to eat before the sun comes up.

"Our doors are to stay open. He sleeps on the floor, and later today, he is to sit down and tell us all he can."

I look over Nate's shoulder at Damon, who is watching Bishop closely. Bishop, who hasn't taken his eyes off me. I ignore him, looking back to Nate, and nod. "Deal."

Nate gets to his feet, holding his hand out to me and helping me up. "Grilled cheese? I can hear your stomach from here."

I exhale, leaning my head on his shoulder, feeling every muscle loosen. "Yes. Fucking God, yes."

Walking out of the closet, I toss Damon the clothes. "Go and get changed. I'll bring you something to eat."

He smiles, taking the clothes and disappearing back into my room. I look at the alarm clock Nate keeps beside his bed, noting the time is 2:00 a.m. Damn, we were really talking that long? When my eyes connect with Bishop's, I mutter, "I've lost my appetite."

Nate pulls me into him. "Naw, don't mind him." He sends Bishop a wink. "He just doesn't like others playing with his toys."

"I'm not his toy."

"I'm right here," Bishop grunts.

"Really?" I say sarcastically. "Because I don't see you."

"Okay, Kitty," Nate chuckles, tucking me under his arm. "You're not you when you're hungry. Let's go."

CHAPTER 16

"OKAY, THAT'S IT," TATUM ANNOUNCES, TRYING to tear into her packet of crackers. "I want to know 100 percent of what is going on. It's not fair!" she whines.

"Don't do that." I rub my temples, still tired after the shit for sleep I got on Saturday night. "I seriously have so much going on right now."

"I know," Tatum whispers, giving up on trying to tear open her pack of carbs. "Remember? I was there."

"There's more. God." I sit back. "There's so much more, but I don't even know where to start and what to tell you because I already know you're going to have more questions. Questions I don't know the answers to." I exhale and open my mouth, just about to continue, when I see the Kings walk into the cafeteria out the corner of my eye. Tatum picks up her unopened crackers again when she sees them all walk in. "Now I *need* carbs."

Bishop takes a seat beside me, and Nate goes on the other side as the rest of the boys squeeze in next to Tatum and Bishop.

"I don't remember calling you over," I snark.

"No need." Nate grins, biting into his apple.

Rolling my eyes, I look back at Tatum to see her staring at something over my shoulder. Her mouth is agape, cracker in the midair.

I inch my head over my shoulder to see what she's looking at when my mouth slams closed. "Excuse me," I murmur, getting off my seat and making my way toward Damon. He's standing there in some of Nate's clothes—loose jeans, black tee, and white high-top sneakers. It's all Nate, since I still haven't found time to get Damon his own.

"What are you doing here?" I ask, watching as everyone stares at him.

What on earth are they staring at? I know he's funny-looking, but now people are just being rude. Or maybe I just think he's funny-looking because he's my brother. I wouldn't know.

"I need to talk to you."

"Talk."

He takes my arm and pulls me back through the girls hallway. Waiting for a couple of people to walk past, his voice drops. "Katsia wants to meet with me."

"What? How do you know?" I whisper back, smiling to a girl who is in my English class as she passes by, looking at us suspiciously.

"Obviously because I've left. Have you read any more of

the book?" he asks urgently.

"No, I haven't found time, and why does she want to meet with you?"

"Find time to read. Because she need me." He pushes off the wall and walks back down the hallway then out the front doors.

"Well goodbye to you too!" I yell toward him as the doors slam shut.

Walking back into the cafeteria, I head to my chair, pulling it out and taking a seat.

"What'd he want?" Bishop inquires beside me.

I ignore him.

"Who is he?" Tatum asks, her eyes searching him out.

"My brother and he's gone."

Her attention snaps to me. "What? How?" She lowers her voice. "Madison...?"

"As I said earlier," I reply, tossing my salad around with my fork, "I have a lot to tell you."

"You're not telling her shit," Bishop snaps, looking at me.

I finally acknowledge him. He's so close—too close to me—that I can almost feel his breath fall over my lips. "And I said you can't tell me what the fuck to do, Bishop."

He chuckles, tossing a carrot in his mouth—*my* carrot. "Oh, Madison. You have no idea the kind of things that tone does to me."

I'm just about to open my mouth to say something else, when Nate interrupts, "Anyway!" He looks between both of us, his eyes wide like he's scolding a couple of toddlers. "Tatum is fine, B. She knows almost everything else that has happened."

"Not everything," I mutter under my breath.

Tatum cuts her glare to me. "Oh? What else don't I know? Hmm?"

Pushing my chair back, I get to my feet, picking up my tray. "I'm done. I'll see you later." Walking out the atrium doors, I make my way toward PE. I'm halfway down the corridor when I decide I don't want to even be at school right now. Turning around, I start heading to the elevator that leads down to the student parking lot when a thought pops into my head. I haven't seen Miss Winters since I've been back.

Turning back around again, I jog toward the library, pushing open the large wooden doors. The smell of dusty old books hits me, and I inhale, relishing in the familiar scent. It has to be my favorite aroma, aside from whatever Bishop wears. Usually. Not right now, because right now I hate him. Bypassing the two quiet students who are studying, I make my way to the front desk.

"Hey!" I smile down at the blonde.

The girl raises her face, and my smile falls. "You're not Miss Winters." I look around. "Where is she?"

"She left about two months ago."

"Left?" I scoff. "Left where?" She can't leave.

"Left, as in doesn't work here anymore, as in I don't know where she is."

I step backward and dash for the doors. I don't know why, but that doesn't sit right with me. Why would Miss Winters leave? Two months ago? That was around when I left. No. She wouldn't leave, and if she did, where has she gone? Pushing my hair out of my face, I jog back to the elevator, pressing the Down button more than what is necessary. The doors finally ding open, and I step inside, pounding on the SP button. The doors close and the elevator takes me down to my car as I think over all the possibilities of where she could be.

Truthfully, I know nothing about her really, but if she was going to leave, I feel like she would have told me the day I got the number from her. Or at the very least hinted. Something's wrong. The doors ding open and I rush to my truck, beeping it unlocked. Opening the door, I'm just about to slide in when something goes over my head, cutting out my vision, and a hand slams over my mouth before picking me up. I scream muffled cries, kicking and turning as he tosses me into what I'm guessing is a van. I go to rip off the... whatever the fuck it is that's over my head, when another pair of hands grab me from behind, wrapping cable ties around my wrists and binding them together.

"Who the fuck are you?" I yell out. I smell her before she speaks though. That rich, unique lemon, rosey-ish scent of Chanel No. 5.

"I just want to talk, Madison."

"Talk?" I laugh. "You fucking kidnap me to talk?" I end my sentence with a screech.

"Take the mask off her please." In an instant, I'm met with Katsia sitting opposite me and looking extremely out of place in her two-piece suit, with two armed men beside her, both wearing ski masks, as well as the guy sitting next to me.

"What do you want to talk about?" I seethe, pissed off. "For the record, I'm usually a pretty easy girl. You can just be like 'Oh, hey, girl! Can we chat?' and I'd be like 'Yeah, for sure, girl! Let's do coffee!'" I act the scene out with bound hand signals and high-pitched tones. My face turns flat when I finish. "You don't need to fucking kidnap me."

She smiles, but it doesn't reach her eyes. I don't think it ever probably has. Unless she's like, having dinner with the devil. Bet the bitch smiles then. "You're funny."

"Thanks," I say sarcastically. "My friends wouldn't agree with you."

"Maybe you need new friends," she retorts, one eyebrow cocked.

"No." I shake my head, seeing where she's going with this conversation. "It's hard enough to find one person who likes me, much less a gang."

She tilts her head, studying me closely. I cringe inwardly at how she regards me with her stare. "What makes you think they do?"

"They do—what?" I ask, matching her stare, scanning over her attire the exact way as she does mine.

She snorts, as if she knows exactly why I did that. "The apple doesn't fall there," she mutters under her breath. I only just catch it.

"What?"

"Another time," she replies.

"No, you were—"

"Another time," she cuts me off, but her smile remains.

This bitch is chilly.

"But tell me," she continues, reaching forward to take a glass of wine from a little table that's set up between the two seats that are facing each other. "What makes you think they actually like you?"

"Well, I don't know. They put up with me."

"That's a terrible answer, Madison." She giggles from behind the rim of her glass. "People put up with a lot of things. Wives, husbands, headaches. Under all that though, is that a way to live? To just put up with someone? No," she shakes her head, taking a sip, "and for the record, you're wrong."

"Wrong about what?"

"Well, that's the kicker." She smirks, her eyes lighting up like a Christmas tree. Oh, this bitch is crazy. "All of it."

"Are you going to fill me in or am I going to be left guessing?" I don't trust her. At all. But am I open to hearing what she has to say? Yes.

"Well, let's start with your brother."

"Let's," I reply, overly excited and a little sarcastic.

She looks at me for a second too long before her eye twitches. "How much do you know about him?"

"Only parts. What he's told me, and what Bishop and Nate have sort of told me."

She laughs. "Mmmm, those boys. I swear, every generation, it happens."

"What?" The confusion must show on my face, because she giggles again. "Oh, Madison. Tell me," she leans forward, "why do you think your father brought you back to The Hamptons?"

That's the question I haven't been able to figure out yet. Why would he bring me back here if he knew it was dangerous for me? "I don't know," I answer honestly. I look directly into her eyes. "Do you?"

She leans back, taking a sip of her wine, all while keeping her eyes locked on mine. "Yes."

"Then will you enlighten me?" I ask her, and she pauses again, looking over my features like she's studying every inch of my face. As if she's fascinated by me.

She leans back. "No. Too soon."

"Too soon?" I scoff. "Are you kidding me? Do you know how much shit I've been through?"

"Oh," she laughs. "I know."

139

"Oh, right." I snort sarcastically. "Because you own the Lost Boys and have for generations. I get it." I roll my eyes for added effect. "Why did you kidnap me anyway?"

"Because I want Damon back."

"Well, by all means, ask him yourself."

She looks at me like I'm stupid. "He won't."

"I wonder why that is."

"Listen to me very carefully, Madison. Damon is a tricky soul. He may be your brother, your twin brother, but he was born…" She looks around, searching for the correct word. "… different."

"Different—how?" I ask, narrowing my eyes. "And why do you say it like you care?"

She smirks. "I care because Damon is very good at what he does. I care because what Damon does is needed. And I care because Damon needs it too, and if Damon doesn't get what he needs, there *will* be a massacre."

"Damon wouldn't hurt a soul."

She chokes on her drink, gripping her throat. "You sweet, deluded child." She leans forward, placing her wine back on the small table. "Damon wouldn't willingly hurt you—no. But, honey, what do you think his name means?"

"I don't know. It's a common boys name."

She shakes her head. "No, the correct spelling of his name is D-A-E-M-O-N, Latin for Son of Satan." I clench my jaw, attempting to fight back any words that are egging to spill out of my gob.

"But I saw how his name was spelled on his shirt. It was spelled D-A-M-O-N."

She rolls her eyes. "His name is bad for business. We had to… citizenize it."

His name was bad for business? Who even says shit like that? "I still don't understand. Daemon is the sweetest guy I know. I was draw—"

She waves her hands around. "Honey, he's not only your brother, but he's your twin. You both felt that—" She connects her hands together. "—pull. But he should never have left. He's been trained by the best of the best. He was supposed to walk away."

"But he didn't," I whisper.

"No," she replies, an eye twitching again. "He didn't. He defied the natural order. He will be punished, but the longer he stays, the worse his punishment will be."

"Well, fuck you then. I would never hand him to you willingly, but even more so now."

She does that smile thing again. "Look, I don't expect you to understand." The van stops and I look out my window to see we're back at the school. My truck door is still open. "Just remember this one thing, Madison." She searches my eyes and I meet hers. "He's not a good man. He's the worst of the worst. You wanna know why?" she asks, tilting her head.

"Why?"

"Because he feels nothing. No remorse, no love, no nothing. Daemon is void of natural human emotions. He does not feel physical pain, nor emotional pain. He was born this way. Then he was trained on top of that. He's a very rare human, but he also suffers from the shadows."

"Like congenital insensitivity to pain?" I ask, still stuck on her first revelation.

She nods, leaning back. "Yes. One in a million get it. It's genetic, you know?" She smirks. "But I know it hasn't run through you."

"His emotional lack of feeling though, is there a condition for that?"

"There are lots of conditions that could trigger it, and truthfully speaking, Daemon probably has all of them." She pauses as if to think over how much she should actually disclose. "Ask him about the shadows, Madison, and then call me. I'm sure you will want to talk." She hands me a card. I look down and read over the gold cardboard with the name Katsia embossed in white and a simple phone number underneath.

The man who is sitting beside me, leans forward, cutting the cable ties off from around my wrist. He slides open the door, and I get out, turning to face her one last time. "Why do you think he can't feel emotions?"

"Because I've seen it, and you will too."

The door closes, and the van takes off in a whoosh, like it wasn't there trying to tear into my life a second ago. Picking my bag up from the ground, I throw it into the truck and get into the driver seat, pushing Start. I spin around in my seat quickly when an eerie chill, a chill as if someone is watching me, creeps up my spine, but I'm met with empty seats.

"I'm losing my mind." I put the car in reverse and drive the fuck out of there.

Mondays.

CHAPTER 17

I'M MAKING A SANDWICH IN THE KITCHEN WHEN "Tequila Sunrise" by Cypress Hill comes blaring through the sound dock. I roll my eyes and pull out my phone, scrolling through my Spotify playlist. Fucking Nate, adding his music to my song list. I shove my phone back into my pocket, giving up and going back to my sandwich. Slamming ham onto my bread, I squirt on some mayonnaise and then add tomatoes, relish, and cheese. The catchy beat catches me off guard, and I start bobbing my head to the beat. I judged a little too soon; this song is actually pretty good.

Taking a massive bite out of my sandwich, my eyes come up to the entry to the kitchen when I see Nate, Bishop, Cash, Brantley, and Hunter standing there watching me. It used to be intimidating, having them in my personal space almost all the time—although this isn't all of the Kings. But now it hardly itches on my skin.

"What?" I ask, chewing my sandwich.

Bishop shakes his head. "Nothing. Where's your brother?"

"Upstairs." I swallow. I haven't had a chance to talk to Daemon about the shadows. Truthfully, I'm a little scared. Because once I ask him, there's no going back. What if his answer changes my view on him? I don't want that. There're many things I want answers to in my life, many things I would sacrifice to get those answers, but Daemon isn't one of them. I feel a strong sense of overprotectiveness when it comes to him, which makes me think… "Am I the younger twin or is he?" Thinking out loud always helps.

Brantley and Cash walk into the kitchen, taking a seat on the bar stools. "You're the older one," Cash answers when he sees no one else is.

"Knew it." I grin, taking another bite.

"Why?" Bishop asks, leaning against the wall.

"Just wondering."

"You're wondering why you feel so protective of him." Bishop takes the words out of my thoughts, pushing off the wall and coming into the kitchen. He pulls open the fridge and takes out a water, twisting the cap off. "He's dangerous, Madison."

I roll my eyes. "If you truly believe that, then why would you let him around me?"

"Well we tried to stop that," Nate interjects. "But good fucking job we did."

"And I said he's dangerous," Bishop finishes. "I didn't say he was dangerous to *you*."

"But the first night you were here, you didn't like him.

144

You almost wanted to kill him."

Bishop laughs, placing the water on the counter. "Almost? There's no such thing as almost when it comes to me, Madison. I don't make mistakes; I make moves. If I do something, you bet your ass I thought about every single thing that had to do with it. I'm not unhinged. I'm calculated. I know exactly what I'm doing when I'm doing it, and you wanna know why that makes me the worst kind of monster?" he asks, though he really doesn't want me to answer, so I stay silent—for once. "Because I've thought about the act over and over again in my head, and every time I asked myself if it was the right thing to do?" He inches closer to me, shoving his hands into his pockets. "It's always a yes. So no, Madison." He leans against the counter. "I don't 'almost' kill anyone. If I want them dead, they will be dead. No matter what."

The word *dead* coming out so close to Daemon's name makes my stomach churn. I place my sandwich down, suddenly losing my appetite.

"Prince Charming obviously." I brush Bishop off.

Brantley laughs. "That's cute. But no, more like a dark knight."

My stomach growls, and I pick up my sandwich again, biting into it. "If you could refrain from hurting my brother, that'd be great."

Bishop looks at me, his eyes sinking into mine. "If he doesn't hurt you—which I don't *think* he will—then deal."

Chewing softly, the front door opens and Elena and my dad walk down the hallway, both pausing when they see the gathering in the kitchen.

"Madison, Nate," my dad greets.

My back straightens as I use the back of my hand to

swipe at my mouth. "Dad! Hey!" I make my way toward him. When I pull him in for a hug, he tenses. "Everything okay?" My dad never tenses with me. Ever. He has always been my rock and always told me what was going on, except when it came to the Kings.

He forces a smile. "Everything is fine."

I look to Elena and she gazes back at me, totally oblivious to what just passed between my dad and me. "Hi, Madi. How was your weekend?" She looks up to Nate. "Come and greet your mother, please." Nate pushes off the wall.

"Of course, Ma." He pulls her in for a bear hug, wrapping one arm around her waist and lifting her off the floor effortlessly. He kisses her on the cheek. "Missed you."

She pulls back, pinching his cheeks. "You're doing just fine, boy. Taking good care of your sister I see." She looks back to me.

"Speaking of," I say to Dad. "Can we talk?"

"What have you done?" he asks Nate, and I quickly interfere. "No, it's nothing like that. Just… something. Can we talk?"

He nods, placing his suitcase down just as Sammy comes through the front door dressed in casual jeans and a knitted sweater.

"Sorry, I wasn't expecting you home until tomorrow." She picks up the bag and winks at me. Huh, Sammy is ultra-happy today, but those questions will have to wait.

Dad gestures toward the hallway. "My office."

Following him down, I step into his space, suddenly engulfed with rich pine, red leather, and ancient books.

He takes a seat on his chair, unbuttoning his suit and removing his tie. It's the first time I've really gotten to look at Dad in a long time. The skin around his eyes sags more than ever, his stubble is a couple days old, and his eyelids look heavy and tired. Just when I'm about to tell him to forget it, not wanting to add to his obviously already stressful life, he opens his mouth. "I realize you have a lot to ask after what happened at Hector's house."

I swallow. "Well, actually, yes and no."

"How much do you know already, Madison?" he whispers hoarsely.

My anger picks up a little. "Why the hell do people keep asking me that? Like they're trying to find a barrier to which they won't cross. Fearing they might say too much, but it's okay for them to say too little. It's deceiving and dishonest."

"Madison," he exhales. "No one is honest in this world. I'm sorry that you're a part of it. I never... we—your mother and I—never wanted you to be a part of this world. It's why we were on the run for so long." He leans back in his chair.

"So why bring me back here then, Dad, if you knew I was in trouble?"

He pauses, running his index finger over his upper lip while he watches me. Probably thinking about whether or not he should be honest with me. Fucking people and their honesty.

"Because...." He leans forward, resting his elbows on the desk. "God, Madison. There is a natural order to how things operate in the Kings. A way that no one has tampered with for generations and generations. Roles that each of us have that we always have had." He pauses, looking up at me from beneath his lids. He exhales again, but I think I've already worked it out.

"You're wanting to change the order."

He looks at me and narrows his eyes. "Yes. But Hector can't know."

I look at him, taking a seat on the chair in front of me. "What do you mean? So why does he think you brought me back?"

He pauses, leans back, and rests his elbow on the arm-rest. Realization comes in. "Wait. Does he think you brought me back to... kill me?"

"What?" my dad exasperates. "Of course fucking not."

Information is swimming around in my head. Information that may as well be in Japanese, because I have no idea what all this means. "Well, can you enlighten me? Because I can't see why else Hector would let me walk free, considering the Kings hid me away to try to make sure he didn't find out I was back here."

Dad's eyes turn to stone, along with his jaw. "That wasn't the whole reason why those boys took you away, Madison. You must never forget who they are, who their loyalty belongs to, because it's not you. It never is to anyone else but to the Hayes men. Must remember that."

I swallow, trying to find the words I want to say. Even though I've been brewing on all my questions for months, now that I can ask my dad anything and he'll probably tell me, I'm coming up dry.

"What does Hector think?" I whisper, glancing out the old wooden window that overlooks our yard.

"He thinks I've come back to send you away with someone."

"Someone?" I ask, whipping my attention back to him. "To who? And why?"

"The Lost Boys, and to be lost."

That brings my attention back into the circle. Into why I'm here. "Well, that's not going to happen."

"What do you mean?" he asks, looking at me sideways.

"Daemon is upstairs and has been here for a few nights now. And before you flip out—he's not dangerous toward me, but I do have questions."

Dad's face falls. He pauses, and then he shoots off his chair like his ass just caught on fire. "What the fuck do you mean he's here?" he roars, his hands flying out. The office door bursts open and Bishop strides in, checking me over quickly before giving my dad a death glare. "She knows he's her brother, her twin," Bishop starts.

"Thanks," I mutter under my breath, turning back in my chair. "I was just getting to that part."

"And that's all she knows."

Hold up. "Wait." I put my hand up. "What does that mean? And why did you just storm into this office like you were afraid my dad was going to say something?" I look back at Dad to see his face soften slightly before eventually falling completely. He looks to me. "Baby girl, go upstairs. I need to talk to Bishop."

"No." I shake my head. "You can talk in front of me."

"The fuck we can. Get your ass upstairs—now." Bishop glares at me.

I wince, but square my shoulders. "Why? Why can't you stop fucking hiding shit from me?"

Bishop takes one step. "Because..." Another step. "You are Madison *fucking* Montgomery..." Step. "The Silver *motherfucking* Swan." Double step. "So get your *fucking* ass upstairs." The tip of his shoe hits mine. "*Now*," he growls.

I run my eyes up his dark jeans, past his clean black shirt, over his thick neck and plump lips, until I'm finally staring into eyes that are like the gates of hell. Only, I would let the fucker push me in and lock them behind him. "One day—" I tilt my head. "—I will know everything, and you won't be able to control shit." I stand, almost nose-to-nose with him.

He looks down at me, his dark glare turning into a grin. "Maybe. Not today though, so get the fuck out."

I turn in my step and walk out of the office before he can yell at me some more. Only he's not yelling at me. Only Bishop has a way about him where it feels like he's yelling at you without actually raising his voice. Must be an intimidation tactic of some sort. He's stella in those.

Taking the stairs one at a time, I walk into my room, slamming the door behind me. Flopping down onto my bed, the fluffy blankets puffing out beneath me, I tilt my head to face the ceiling as I replay over all the new information. I know I'm not going to get anything solid out of anyone around here.

"Madison…," Daemon whispers softly.

I keep my vision locked on the ceiling. "Yes, Daemon?"

"The book."

Pushing myself up, I reach under the bed and search for the book. Something has happened with Miss Winters too. How has she disappeared? And Tillie. Where the fuck is Tillie? There's so much I still have to figure out, but for some reason, I feel like my answers will lie between the words in this book, not by trying to decipher the Latin language from my long lost twin brother.

Fuck this book.

Flicking open the page, I sink into my bed and continue where I left off.

12.
The birth of the Lost Boys

One... Two... Three... Four... Five... Six...
I counted each head. "Why are you here?" I asked, tilting my head at Joshua. Joshua was the first person to put his hand up when Humphrey decided to cook up this idea. Why? I don't know. Humphrey comes from a good home. I thought he was a good kid too.
"Because I want to do something useful with my life. Make my family proud."
"Proud?" I asked. "Proud of killing innocent babies? Because that's what you will be doing."
He swallowed, and I saw his jaw flinch. "I—I don't. I will do what I need to do, ma'am."
"What if I gave you another job? Something that will still make your family proud but won't have you doing such disturbing jobs." I pushed off the counter and walked toward him. "I'm offering you an ultimatum, Joshua. Will you accept it?"
He looked deep into my eyes, and I saw it. I saw his silent cries for help. The way the corner of his eyes crinkled when I offered him a different job. "I will do anything, Miss Katsia. I think that much is obvious."
I nodded then come-hithered the other five boys who were waiting patiently for me at the back of the empty cave. "Who knows about fireflies?"
They all stepped forward, shaking their head. "Not much," one of them replied. This one was strong. I could see it in how his shoulders squared with self-assurance and the way he didn't flinch.
"Well," I began. "What do you know about beetles?"

They all shook their heads.

"Okay, so what's more appealing? The firefly or the beetle?"

"Firefly," they all murmured, looking at each other for approval.

I smiled. "But did you know that the firefly is still only a beetle? They're just nocturnal members of the family."

"What's your point, Miss Katsia?" the cocky boy asked, and I admire his no beating around the bush attitude. He's going to need it.

"My point is, how they see us..." I pointed out toward the outside of the cave. "Has to be the beetle. We have to remain within the same family. They have to think we're of the same family. Fighting for the same cause."

"But we're not going to be—are we?" Joshua whispered, looking to me in awe.

I shook my head slowly, a small smile tickling my lips. "No."

"So what would you be having us do, Katsia?" the cocky boy asked.

Looking back to him, I tilted my head. "What's your name?"

"Benjamin."

"Benjiman... who?"

"Benjiman Vitiosus."

"Ahhh," I mumbled. It made sense. He was a Vitiosis. I didn't recognize him earlier because the order of the Lost Boys worked like this: If you're a sibling who doesn't have what they call Elite Blood, then you get thrown in to be a Lost Boy, who—what Humphrey wants to do—are cleaners of the world. Humphrey has lined out the world very thoroughly. We have breeding time, which is the only time that we can try for babies. If you don't fall pregnant, then you will have to wait four years before you can try again, and you only get to try

twice. You see, Humphrey has made a natural order in the most unnatural way. You get the first two tries, and then you cannot try again. It's about breeding them, but we need them in fours. Humphrey was too smart for his own good, for all of us. He had everything mapped out, and no one was stopping him. Not now—not ever.

If you had a child or a nephew who didn't have Elite Blood, meaning they didn't have what it took to be a King, then they got thrown in to be a Lost Boy. Trained. Well, that was what I was supposed to be doing, but instead, I have another plan for these boys. I want to fight Humphrey. Fight his cause and fight it to the death. He took my baby girl and killed her. Now… now I start a very detailed plan to kill him.

Slamming the book closed, I think over what I just read. I'm beginning to see the shift in Katsia from what she was in the beginning. She's stronger. There's vengeance in her blood, and we all know that once vengeance seeps into your blood, there's no extracting that from your system. The only way that gets siphoned out is by getting your revenge. So all Lost Boys are somehow intertwined into the family of one of the Kings. This world is, once again, messed up. Flipping over, I hit my light and slide under my covers, snuggling into my warm sheets and drifting into a deep sleep.

Fog from the empty night expels from my lungs, and I stop running, leaning over to catch my breath. "Riddle me this, Kitty."

"NO!" I scream, shielding my ears with my hands. "Fuck you!" Slamming my eyes closed, I shoot forward, the damp leaves sliding under the soles of my shoes. My heart pounds in my chest and my blood tears through my veins like bullets full of adrenalin. I keep running blindly as sweat trickles down my cool flesh, goose bumps breaking out over my spine, so I open my eyes and stop. Looking out to the still lake in the middle of the forest, I whisper in confusion, "What?"

I spin around to try to figure out where I just came from, but nothing is there. Only the bushes that hide the lake—the same lake Bishop and I fooled around in. A single bright firefly flutters in the air, swimming around in front of my face. I smile, letting the little bug light something inside of my gut. Reaching out, I go to touch it, but just as my fingertip connects with the little body, it turns to blood, dripping down over my finger.

"Ew!" I pull my finger back then look around the empty lake again. "Why am I here?" Wind whisks through my hair, igniting my skin and senses, and that's when I smell it—the sweet, soapy scent of man. Inching my head over my shoulder, I smile softly.

"Took you long enough."

Bishop steps forward so he's standing directly beside me and looks out to the lake. "You run faster now."

I grin, turning to face him. "Or you've gotten slower." Looking him up and down, I take in what he's wearing and my eyebrows pull together in confusion. He has no shirt on, his delicious body on full display, and his ripped jeans cover his long, lean legs. Barefoot, standing there like that in the middle of almost winter seems ridiculously strange. Actually, this entire setting feels strange. I look out toward the rock

Bishop and I played around on what feels like years ago now, and smile. "There's that rock." When he doesn't answer, I turn to face him, but he's gone.

"Bishop?" I call out, looking around for him. Something doesn't feel right. Actually, everything feels extremely wrong.

"Kitty," Nate murmurs, and I spin around, seeing Nate leaning on his elbows in the sand, with no shirt on either.

"Aren't you cold?" I ask him, finally having enough of all the lack of clothes.

"I don't know." Nate runs his eyes up and down my body then grins. "Aren't you?"

"No, I...." I look down to see I'm wearing nothing but a little black G-string and a black bra. "Oh my God!" But he's right. I'm not cold.

"Nice. Can see why you're both hitting that." Brantley's dark voice comes in from the shadows behind Nate.

"Bishop, yes. Nate, no," I correct, my hands on my hips.

"Nate, almost—twice." Nate smirks.

I open my mouth, just about to correct him again, when Hunter, Jase, Ace, Saint, Eli, Cash, and Chase slowly come in behind Brantley, all similarly dressed.

"The gang's all here?" I ask, shaking my head.

Nate glares over my shoulder, his eyes going dark. "Now they are."

A hand runs up my thigh while another grips onto my hip, holding me into place. I close my eyes. "Bishop...."

His lips skim over my shoulder, his breath falling on my cool skin. "Who owns you?" Then he licks me from shoulder blade to shoulder blade while his hand on my thigh travels up to my apex. "Who owns you, Madison?"

I moan out slightly, biting down on my bottom lip.

He squeezes. "I'm not a patient man."

"Why?" I ask. Even in the midst of my lust, my stubborn ass still can't let some shit go.

His fingertips dig into the flesh of my thigh. "Say it. Tell me what I want to hear," he growls, his lips pressing against the rim of my earlobe.

"You."

Shit.

He chuckles into my ear. "Good." His hand sprawls over my stomach. "Because you're about to get fucked like I don't."

Wait, what?

I turn to face him, confused. When he sees my puzzlement, he grins and looks over my shoulder. Another hand comes to the front of my throat and squeezes down.

Shit. Double shit.

Why does everything feel so good? Bishop drops to his knees in front of me as whoever it is behind me grips onto my throat, tilting my head to the side as his teeth latch onto my neck.

"You want this and you know it."

Brantley.

Fuck.

Bishop tears my G-string off, and I look down at him as he brings it up to his face and inhales deeply. "Mine."

I want to kick him and say, *If I'm yours, then why are you sharing me?* but everything feels too good. Like I'm floating on a cloud of ecstasy.

I feel no shame.

Then Bishop draws his tongue out and runs it over my panty line, a devilish smirk coming to his mouth as his eyes light up like fire. Then he hooks my G-string over his neck and wears it like a damn necklace.

Jesus Christ, is he kidding?

Brantley's hand comes up to my bra and cups my boob, squeezing roughly just as the cool air that was whisking past my clit is replaced with Bishop's warm mouth. "Oh my God!" I groan, my head tilting back and hitting Brantley's chest. Brantley tears off my bra and pinches my nipples as Bishop's tongue circles my clit, switching between rough and gentle.

"Lay down," Brantley murmurs into my ear.

"What?" I'm still coming out of my daze when he wraps my hair around his fist and yanks me down to the sand. "Lay the fuck down." I fall onto my ass, and both him and Bishop look down at me sprawled out on the ground.

"Well, damn," a third voice says, coming into view.

Saint. Cash's older brother.

He unbuttons his jeans and I gulp. Holy shit. He has six years on all of us.

"Scared?" he asks, rubbing his hand over his dick. I watch as the muscles in his chest flex. His angular jaw tenses and I look at him with fresh eyes. Or horny eyes—either one. He has a sprinkling of hair over his jaw, groomed perfectly. His nose is a little wider, but his skin is golden and his hair blond. He sort of looks like that actor Cam Gigandet, I've decided. He nudges his head. "You good with this?"

I want to say no. I should say no. Shit. I don't want to say no. Nodding, I slowly pull my bottom lip into my mouth. *What a fucking whore.* He gets down to his knees and Bishop and Brantley both step aside, parting like the Red Sea to let him in.

"You gon' purr tonight."

He pushes his jeans down, tugging on his cock a few

times, and then lays over me. I drop to my back, my arms going out, giving him access. His bulky body weighs on me as the tip of his thick cock presses at my entrance before slipping in, thanks to Bishop's foreplay. My eyes pop open and I arch my back, letting out a moan loud enough to shake the trees.

He grins against my cheek. "That's not even half, baby. I'm going to break you." Then he pulls out and flips me onto my stomach, grabbing one leg and hitching it onto his hip as he dives inside me again. The way the tip of his cock collides with my cervix says I'm taking it all. Hands wrap around my hair and I look up the best I can to see Bishop. He unzips his jeans, pulling them down enough until his cock springs free, and then he lies back on the sand, leaning back on his elbows. Biting down on his bottom lip, his hair slightly ruffled and his eyes weak with lust, he nods down at his cock. "You know what to do, baby." Putting my weight on one hand, I grip his dick with my other hand, sliding my lips over his head, and swallow him deeply. Bobbing up and down, I swirl my tongue around him and take him deeper until he's hitting the back of my tonsils. He looks directly at me as Saint dives into me over and over again, hitting some sweet spot hidden deep inside me. I pause my sucking, swinging my hair over one shoulder, and look up to Bishop. He moves some of my hair out of my face sweetly, smirks, and then wraps it around his fist, tugging my face up to look at him more.

"Nate!" he calls out, his eyes not moving from me. Saint withdrawals from me, taking all my pleasure and buildup with him.

"Yo!" Nate answers. I can't see where he is, but I'm guessing he's right behind me—with a great view.

"Tell me how good she tastes."

I narrow my eyes at Bishop and open my mouth to protest, but his grip tightens and I flinch, my eyes slamming closed. "Who owns you?" he growls.

"But—"

"Shut the fuck up. Who owns you?" I open my eyes, tears creeping out of the corners. Tears from my hair almost getting ripped out, or tears from the feelings of abandonment I've started to sense deep in my chest. He doesn't care. I really am just a trick to him. A game. If he cared, I wouldn't be getting tossed around like public property. Before I can blink, I'm angry. Angry at him, but turned on by that anger.

"You own me, Bishop." I give him what he wants while ignoring the stabbing feeling I feel in my throat.

"Now, spread them open and let him in."

I look up at Nate and he smirks at me. "Promise to be gentle."

I roll my eyes, because as far as I know, Nate isn't nearly as ruthless as Brantley and Bishop, so that's the least of my issues. Nate leans down, placing a kiss on my lips. I lean into him, his mouth meshing with mine.

"Kitty," he whispers against my lips.

Something pokes into my chest, and I turn from left to right, not wanting this kiss to stop. Nate does kissing well.

"Kitty…."

There's that prodding again. What the fuck? In an instant, the front of my belly has been doused in water and ice prickles over my nipples.

I shoot off the bed, reality slowly seeping its ugly fucking claws deep inside of me. "Fuck!" Rubbing my eyes, I look down at the front of my shirt, seeing my pajama top is soaked through. "Double fuck!" Then I look up, seeing Nate standing next to my bed with a water bottle in his hand and a grin on his face.

"You!" I narrow my eyes and slowly start to crawl down the bed, like a tiger about to eat its prey. I'm about to eat my prey—that prey being Nate.

"No," he retreats, his hands coming up in surrender. "That's not what…. I was waking you up because…." He looks around my room, trying to find a valid excuse. Squaring his shoulders, his face turns serious. "Imagine if the house was on fire, Mads!"

"But it's not. Is it?" I challenge, standing to my feet. I watch him, and he looks over to my bedroom door briefly before looking back to me. "Madi, I can explain. It's…." Then he makes a dash for it, launching toward my bedroom door and slamming it behind him. I fly toward it, twisting on my door handle and banging on the wood. "Open this fucking door, Nate!" I scream.

"No! Say you won't, like, hurt my balls or something."

"I won't fucking hurt you!"

"Lies!" he yells back. "I know when you're lying, because you add a 'fucking' in the middle. Tell me the truth!"

Exhaling in defeat, I open my mouth, just about to surrender, when I see my bathroom door open. Grinning, I slowly step backward. "Okay, I'm sorry. Do you forgive me?" Silently, I step into the bathroom, slide over to his door, and twist the handle open. It's unlocked. Grinning from my cleverness, I pull the door open, but my face falls instantly.

"Going somewhere?" Bishop is standing in front of me, shirtless with those ripped jeans on. He basically just walked right out of my dream. Life is not fair and the universe obviously fucking hates me.

"I-uh…" I look around the room, hitching my thumb over my shoulder. "…am just going to go." I spin around and start to run back toward my room, but Bishop hooks his arm around my waist, lifting me off the ground and throwing me over his shoulder like I weigh nothing.

"Bishop!" I yell. "Put me the fuck down!"

"Ah, see… you put a 'fuck' in there. You must be mad." He slaps my ass cheek, the sting vibrating over my skin. "Calm yourself, woman!"

"I hate you!" I shriek, just as he throws me onto my bed. The morning sun glaring through my porch windows catches his messy bed hair. The chestnut brown color sets off the contrast of his tanned skin.

His eyes turn almost black. "Yeah? Well, I don't give a fuck. You've hated me for so long now."

"This is different!" I shout back, suddenly angry at him.

"What?" He matches my level of loud. Spreading his arms out, he smirks. "How? How is this different?"

"You let Saint fuck me and Nate go down on me!" I scream, tears suddenly slipping down my cheeks. Jesus. When did I become such a girl? I make a mental note to check the dates, because I must be due for Mother Nature's visit. There's no way I'm this much of a pussy-ass bitch.

Bishop stops. His eyes look straight into mine, commanding the entire room while summoning my fucking soul. Because that's what he does. When his stance changes to this one—one I've only seen twice now—he stares into my eyes and summons my soul. But with my soul come my demons, and I think that's the part he's only just figuring out.

"Come again," he growls softly. Too softly.

I shiver in fear, because I should be fucking scared. Every survival instinct the human body has is on high alert within me right now. Run. I should run. But I can't, because he's fucking summoned me. Because—

"Madison," he repeats in the same tone, cocks his head a little, and slowly walks toward the foot of my bed. "Repeat what you just said, and think very carefully about your next words, because my fingers are twitching to snap some necks…" He pauses, breaking our eye contact and glaring right at my throat. "…and yours is looking rather snapable too."

Oh shit.

"Okay, hang on." I stand up from the bed, feeling more confident on my feet. "I meant that—" He pushes me back down onto the bed. "Bishop!" I yell, propping myself up on my elbows and looking up at him.

"Did any of them touch you?"

"Bishop—"

He grips onto my leg and pushes me up my bed, stepping between my thighs. "Don't, Madison. Don't fuck with this."

"I meant it was—"

He presses his lips to the crook of my neck and bites down on it roughly.

"Was what?" he asks, his voice vibrating against my skin as his other hand comes up to my throat. His thumb caresses my jawline gently as he kisses and licks all over my neck. Biting down on my bottom lip to fight a moan, I close my eyes, but then he presses his dick into me, and I lose it.

"Was a fucking dream!" I yell, still slightly angry at him.

He stops, pauses, and settles his face into my neck. Seconds pass when I feel his body jerking on top of me.

Narrowing my eyes, I slap him in the ribs. "Are you fucking laughing?"

Then he bursts into fits of laughter, rolling onto his back while clutching his stomach. "Fuck."

I'm staring at him, confused and annoyed, and just when I'm about to hit him again, I realize this is the first time I've ever seen Bishop laugh. Or even smile this big. Or just smile without there being an ulterior motive behind it.

Before I can stop myself, I giggle. "Stop laughing. It's not funny."

He slams his mouth closed as he tries to contain his fit, and then he looks to me, his eyes dancing with humor. "Sorry, babe. But that's fucking hilarious. You getting mad at me over a dream."

"Stop. It was more than that, and it felt like...."

He hooks his arm around my waist, lifts me up, and puts me on top of him so I'm straddling his waist. Placing his arms behind his head, he stares at me, so I look away, scared he'll summon some more of my soul and never give it back. "Hey," he whispers. "Look at me."

I shake my head. "I sort of don't want to."

"Why?" he whispers again, and I know in his tone that he's being honest.

"Because."

"Because why, Madison?"

"Because you steal some of my soul every time you do that thing with your eyes."

He slams his mouth closed again, his stomach jerking beneath me.

Oh no he is—

"Are you laughing at me again?" My eyes snap to his and

163

he bursts out laughing once more. I go to get off him when he grabs me around the waist again and pulls me down so my lips are within an inch of his. "Hey," he repeats, his warm breath falling over my lips. "Look at me."

Knowing he will never let up, I look at him. I mean, eyes a little crossed, front row seating, soul clenching, really look at him, and my heart launches in my chest. *That's* what needs to get summoned… right the fuck out of my body.

"What?" I meant for my tone to be harsher than what it is when it comes out.

"I'd never fucking share you. Period. Yes, we fuck around a bit, but the boys know there's a line when it comes to you, and if any of them cross it, I have no problem being a King short."

I laugh, shaking my head. He can't mean that. We fight so much; he's never told me how he's felt—only maybe once before, outside my house—but I never know when he's being truly sincere, because everything is always a game. And I usually always lose. This, though, the way he's looking at me and how he's talking to me, it's putting dents in my solid plan to get revenge.

"I know what you're doing." His fingers dig into my hips.

"Oh?" I ask, pushing off his chest so I'm sitting on him properly. "And what exactly is that?"

He smirks. "You wanted to get revenge on me. On all of us. Hell, I knew that a long time ago. Why do you think I never came to get you back from overseas when I could have?"

"What do you mean?"

"I mean, you think I didn't know you were in New Zealand? That you used to sit at that little black table and draw for the tattoo artist, Jesse? That you started having a little thing for him? I knew everything, Madison. There wasn't a second when you weren't under my protection."

I blink, and try to gather enough coherent thoughts to ask some questions.

"How? But why didn't you get me then?"

"There was stuff going on here that needed to be cleaned up, and you needed to calm down. I would've rather had you out of the US while everything was getting sorted."

"Did it get sorted?" I ask, wiggling up his body so I'm away from his dick.

"No." He pushes me back down so now I'm directly on top of it.

Shit.

"So why did you bring me back?" I try to shuffle off, annoyed at how horny it makes me with him pressed against me like that. And aside from the fact I am angry about that dream, it turned me on the same.

He pulls down on me, hard enough for me to hiss. Narrowing his eyes, his other hand comes up, and he hooks his finger under my chin, tilting my head up. "Someone touched what is mine. That's what the fuck happened."

"You say that, yet you don't tell me what 'we' are, or anything."

"A label? You want a label?"

"No!" I shake my head. Exhaling, I get off his lap, and he lets me. "I don't know what I want, but I know I want you."

"Well fuck the rest of it. That's all that matters."

"But what does this mean?" I ask, gesturing between the two of us, my girl brain ticking at a hundred miles an hour.

"It means you're mine. That's all that means."

"And... what about you?" I laugh sarcastically. "If you

think I'm going to watch as you go around—"

"Have you ever seen me be a slut?"

"I've seen you touch one," I mutter under my breath, remembering him and Ally. My tone is 100 percent salty and not a single fuck is given.

He doesn't reply, so I look up at him. He's standing in front of me, his knees leaning against the mattress of my bed. Bending down, he spreads my legs open and steps between them. Leaning down, he runs his lips over mine. "And she's dead. So I'll ask you again, have you seen me be a slut?"

The way he talks about Ally being dead—and the fact he's the one who killed her—should upset me, but it doesn't. I don't know why he did it. Hell, I don't even understand what Ally could have done to deserve being knocked off. But for some crazy reason, I don't care.

"No." I shake my head slowly, and he leans down again, pressing a kiss against my lips. My bedroom door swings open. "So, that was—" Nate stops, and Bishop smiles against my lips before stepping backward. "Did I interrupt something?"

"Go away. Please go away," I laugh at Nate.

"Well now, you've just made it more exciting for me to stay." He walks in and sits beside me on my bed, a Cheshire grin on his face.

"Motherfucker."

His grin deepens.

"I've got shit to sort anyway. I'll see you at school," Bishop announces, looking at me briefly before walking out the door, back into Nate's room.

"Put a shirt on!" I yell toward his retreating back, and he chuckles slightly, closing the door behind him.

"So!" Nate turns to me, putting his hands together like a little girl excited that she just got invited to a sleepover. "Tell me all the goss'!"

"Fuck you." I roll my eyes and get off the bed.

His shoulders sag. "You're no fun."

I walk into my closet and flick the light on. "Let's just say," I murmur, scanning through my skinny jeans, "he's finally claimed me." I settle for the black ones with rips in the knees. Pulling down a tight, V-neck, long-sleeved shirt, I turn to face Nate when he's silent.

He's smiling. Like I knew he would be. "He claimed you that first day you walked into Riverside, Kitty. You're gonna have to give me more than that."

Removing my clothes, I tug on my jeans… then tug some more, because apparently I've put on weight, and then button them up. "No, but it's… I don't know… different now. There's so many layers to Bishop. I never know when he's actually being truthful." Throwing on my shirt, I pull my hair out of the back and fluff it up.

"Well…" Nate begins, standing from the bed and walking toward me. "When it comes to real shit, I mean shit he cares about—which is pretty much nothing, aside from you—you're safe. I can vouch for that, Kitty." He pulls some loose strands out from under my shirt. "He won't hurt you."

"Promise?" I ask, looking into his eyes.

Nate nods. "I promise."

CHAPTER 18

Unlocking my truck, I slide into the driver seat, as Nate gets into the passenger, deciding he doesn't want to drive today. "How's Daemon?" he asks, pushing buttons on the radio.

"He's okay. Katsia wants him back and is demanding a meeting with him, but I want to be there."

Nate looks straight at me. "You're not going anywhere without the Kings, and you damn well know that."

"No, look, I need to handle this on my own. I read a bit about the Lost Boys last night, and I just…. I have questions I need answered, and I know if you guys are there, she's less inclined to give me those answers. So please." I look to him, putting the car in drive. "Just let me handle this on my own."

He doesn't fight, just shrugs and hits Play on Kendrick

I laugh, shaking my head as I pull out of our driveway. "I swear you were living in the hood in your past life."

"Tsk tsk." Nate shakes his head. "Don't stereotype." He starts bobbing his head to the beat and raps out the chorus. Laughing, he waves his hand. "Come on… rap it with me…."

Shaking my head, I turn onto the main highway that leads to school. "No thanks."

School is boring, and I truly feel like I'm over it. "At least this is our last year," I mutter to Tatum.

"True!" she agrees, shoving books into her locker. I pause, thinking about the order Katsia spoke about in the book. So if we're all leaving for college, then that means there's a new group of Kings that are going to be starting next year. I need to call Daemon. Pulling my phone out of my pocket, I shut my locker and press Call on his name. He picks up almost instantly, his voice soothing like hot chocolate on a cool winter day.

"Are you okay?" he asks, curt, straightforward, and blunt, but it's Daemon, and from how short I've known him, you don't usually get any other tone.

"Yes, but hey, I need to talk to you about something. Are you home?"

"I am."

"Okay, be ready and I'll pick you up."

"See you then," he replies with the same tenor, hanging up.

"Jeez," Tatum murmurs beside me. "His tone? Does he hate the world?"

Her assumption annoys me. Daemon is a lot of things, some things not even I completely know yet. "No," I snap.

"He's just… different."

She shrugs, and we both start walking toward the elevator. "Different, as in Ted Bundy and Jack the Ripper different, or different, as in 'I draw naked in the moonlight' different?"

I roll my eyes, pushing the button to take us down. "Probably more on the Jack the Ripper side, I'm guessing," I murmur, and she looks at me.

"No way."

"I said probably, not definitely. Anyway, keep your paws off him."

"Hey!" She throws her hands up, and we step into the car. "I don't want to be another victim. I'll stay away."

She won't stay away.

We get into the truck and I put it into reverse. "I'll drop you off. I just need to have this conversation with Daemon alone."

"Are you going to tell me what is going on?" she asks. She didn't ask in an entitled tone. It was more in a way as if she's worried and wants to know everything is okay. Which is Tatum. She's outgoing, blunt, a little flirty, and a lot sassy, but she's real. She's always kept it real with me, and she will forever be my best friend.

I exhale. "I am. Just… give me some time?" I look at her briefly as I pull out onto the main road.

"Okay," she nods, "I can do time."

Driving up to my house, I beep the horn, deciding to wait in the car for Daemon. He comes walking out in a dark suit, buttoned up at the front.

"Huh!" I look at him as he slides into the passenger seat. "You go shopping?"

He looks down at his clothes and then back to me, his eyes expressionless. "Yes."

Pulling out of the driveway, I turn to him slightly. "This talk, can we do it in English?"

He nods. "Yes. I might be little slow, but yes."

I smile and turn the radio on. "Jungle" by Tash Sultana starts playing, and I hit it up a notch. I love this artist. She's from Australia and completely underground, but her voice is soulful and her music touches you deeply.

"Are you okay?" I ask Daemon when he doesn't say anything.

He nods, unbuttoning his jacket. "Yes. What do you want to talk about?"

I shuffle around in my seat. "Katsia, mainly, and the Lost Boys. And also, the next generation of Kings. Is that going to be okay for you?"

He nods again. "That's fine. The next generation of Kings isn't so easy to..." He pauses, looking for the word he wants to use. "...explain. They are..." He looks to me again. "...hidden. Unknown as to what the next move is or if they are starting."

Well, that makes entirely no sense, but we continue driving until I come to the turn off to the forest we went through on Halloween. Pulling down the long stretch of road—the road that is so much less scary than it is at night—and follow it right to the end.

"I know this place," Daemon announces, a little sketchy.

"You do?" I answer, turning into the little parking lot.

"Yes." He looks at me, confused. "How do you know this place?"

"Well, long story short, a friend threw a party here."

"A party?" he asks again.

I pause with my hand on the door handle. "Yes, you know...." I gesture up to my mouth as in drinking, and then boogie in my seat as in dancing.

He looks at me, bored, not catching any of my hints.

"Well this is going to be a long chat then," I mutter, getting out of the car. He follows, shutting the door, and I lock it.

I'm just about to walk toward the clearing, when he grabs onto my arm, tugging me back. I look down at his grip and then back to his face. "What's wrong?"

Shaking his head, he whispers, "You should not have been here, Madison. This isn't your place."

"My place?" I step toward him. "What do you mean? It's beautiful here."

"Something is wrong." He searches the forest and then looks back to me. "Get back in the car and do it slowly."

"What?" I look around the area but don't move my head—making it less obvious. "What do you mean?"

"Don't ask questions. Just do it."

Searching his eyes, I can see him pleading with me. "Okay." Slowly, I sidestep and walk toward the driver door, beeping the alarm system and sliding in. Daemon stays in the same spot, his shoulders square and his stance in fighting mode. It sends chills down my spine, and my fear kicks up to inhumane levels. Pulling the door open, I'm about to slide in when it hits. A sharp sting stabs me right in the head, and I'm falling.

Looking up, the tips of the trees are coming in and out in a distant view. Ringing starts piercing my ears, and I tilt my head as the sun blares right down on my face. Daemon is there, but his face is blurry, and he's yelling at me. Why's he yelling? Why am I on the ground? *Am* I on the ground?

Daemon's eyes are furious, almost black. There's spit flying out of his mouth as he screams at me, but I can't hear anything because I'm deafened by the ringing in my ear.

I laugh because this is the first time I've ever seen Daemon out of control. Why is he so intractable? He wouldn't be like this unless something was extremely wrong. Metallic liquid floods my throat, and I start to panic. My heart launches in my throat as my airways start to slowly clench, making breathing damn near impossible.

Daemon is like this because something *is* wrong. So terribly wrong. I look back at him, bringing my hands to my throat, wanting to rip off my skin to give myself air to breathe, but it's no use. Daemon looks down at me, his eyes pained and his face strained.

Why's he got blood all over him?

Is that my blood?

That's when it hits me.

I'm dying.

CHAPTER 19

Daemon

THE VOICES.
One.
Two.
Three.
Four.
Five.
Six…
Six…
Six….

"She belongs to us. To the dark. Don't put her in the light. She'll burn there, Demon. Don't put her in the light. It's bad for her. Bad, bad, bad. She needs to be where we are, in the dark. Hidden, where it's quiet. Where no one can hurt her."

"No, don't kill her! She's special... so special. Look at her. She's beautiful."

"Shut up!" I roar, banging my fists against my head. "They... they won't stop!" I look down at Madison. Sweet Madison. My sister. My twin. The only person I've ever felt for. The only human I've ever felt a connection with.

"Connection?" The voice snickers. *"The only connection is you know you're supposed to kill her. You know it, so do it. Kill her. She's already dying. Hell, she might even be dead."*

Sucking in a breath, I look down at Madison's body. Her tiny frame unmoving and still. What have I done?

I did this.

She shouldn't have been here.

Grabbing the mobile device Madison gave me, I dial 911. I'm not completely clueless, it's a part of my job as a civilian to know emergency services number. I do not care about the Kings right now. She needs medical help, and I don't know who they use. I trust no one. "Trust no one. Trust no one...."

"Nine-one-one, what is your emergency?"

"Trust no one."

"Sir?"

I clutch my phone tightly, pressing it against my ear. Biting down on my fist, the metallic tinge of blood hits my taste buds, and I recoil. I've done bad things. Very bad things in my lifetime. Unspeakable things. But they're all I know. I've swum in the blood of innocents and drank from their soul without flinching. But this is Madison. My sister. My twin. I care about her.

"You don't care about her," the voice laughs. *"You care because you want to kill her. Imagine what it would be like slicing into that delicate skin."*

175

"Shut up!" I scream, slamming my eyes closed.

"Sir?"

"I need help," I speak, though my English is not very good. "My sister. She's hurt."

"Okay, where are you?"

I look around. "I'm at the clearing on State Highway 50."

"Okay, sir, I have someone on the way. Tell me what's wrong with your sister."

I look down at her and freeze. Her skin is pale, the blood still oozing.

"She's hurt so very bad."

"Okay, I get that, but is she breathing? How is she hurt?"

"She…." I lean down, pressing my two fingers to the side of her neck. A faint pulse taps against the pads of my fingers. Distant, but there—only just. "Her pulse is slow… so very slow."

"Finish her," one of the voices snarks.

"Tace!" I order. My shoulders square, the dark spell coats my flesh, and my lip curls. He's here. It's here. *"Ego sum magister vester!"*

The voices, all five of them, run, slithering in fear. *"Yes, yes you are our master."*

Reality gets sucked back into view, and I'm standing there, clutching my phone while the paramedics are working on Madison. Everything goes in slow motion, and I drop my phone, falling to my knees and clutching my head. What happened?

What happened?

Why do I feel like this is my fault?

Stretching my arms wide, an earth-shattering scream erupts out of me as tears pour out of my eyes. I've never lost control. Never. I'm always in control. Nothing touches me. I don't feel. I don't feel anything. But seeing Madison motionless on the ground, it's like I suddenly feel everything.

"Sir!" A paramedic comes rushing over, blood on his hands. "What happened?"

My chest heaves as I take in deep breaths, my head hanging between my shoulders in defeat. I slowly look up at him and snarl, "She shot in the head."

CHAPTER 20

Madison

B*EEP.*
  Beep.
  Beep.

Pain.

Beep.

Feels like a thousand bricks are weighing down on my head.

Beep.

I try to wiggle my toes, only they don't move. I don't think they move. Where am I?

Beep.

I strain to open my eyes, but not sure whether they're

A voice! Whose voice is that?

Beep.

I'm so tired. Like sinking sand, I feel my consciousness slowly detach itself from wherever I am. The beeping sounds distant now.

Beep.

"Did you try to kill her?" is the last distant thing I hear before the depths of nothingness envelop me completely.

My throat throbs, like I've swallowed gallons of sand. Moving my head slightly, I groan. My head pounds like a bass line is vibrating directly through my brainwaves. It's almost too painful to bear. Wiggling my fingers, this time I feel them respond and someone grabs my hand beside me.

"Madison?"

Who is that? Slowly, I open my eyes. Heavy and tired, like glue has set on my eyelashes, but I stubbornly fight it.

"Water," I urge, still not knowing who that is. There's a straw pressing against my lips, hitting the cracks. I open my mouth a little, enough to fit the tiny straw in and suck. The water is warm, but it slides down my parched throat perfectly. Moving my head back after drinking all of it, I wince.

"Hurts."

"I know, babe."

"Who is this? I can't see."

"Open your eyes, babe."

I fight for it, God knows I do, and when my eyes finally open, my eyebrows pull in. "Tillie?" She looks the same from what I remember, only I'm seeing three of her, and her voice is echoing in and out.

"It's me, but I can't stay long." Her words reverberate, and

I can slowly feel the familiar sinking sand slide out from under me.

No!

"Tillie…." I want it to come out excitedly, happy that she's here, but it comes out more like pain.

"I'm sorry, Madison." She kisses me somewhere on my head. "I had to make sure you were okay, but I have to go now."

"Go?" I mutter. "No! You just got here." I peel my eyes open a little wider, but she's still blurry. "Please don't leave."

"I have to. It's not safe for me here."

"Tell me, Tillie," I croak out. "I can keep secrets. Please."

"I know you can, Mads. But I can't. I just can't. I have to go. I love you."

"Tillie!" I groan, and as she snatches up her hoodie and heads to the door, she turns over her shoulder to face me. "I'm sorry." Then she leaves. I rest my head back, ignoring the excruciating pain.

"Madison?" Bishop murmurs, but I can't see him.

"Bishop?" I gasp, looking around the room for him. I look to the corner and see the outline of his body, the tip of his white sneakers glowing from the moonlight peering in. He's leaning forward, his elbows resting on his knees. "Did you see that?"

He chuckles. "It's amusing you think I'd let any motherfucker near you. Of course I saw that. I allowed it."

"Oh," I murmur, wincing at the pain. I want to ask why he allowed Tillie in, but I sense he won't tell me anything right now.

"You okay?" He gets up from his chair and walks toward me. He's in his usual clothes, looking like he always does—perfect. But when he leans down and places a kiss on my head, I see him closer. He has bags under his eyes like he hasn't slept in days.

"What happened?" I whisper, confused by my choppy memories. "All I remember is… pain."

I wince again, and he pushes the button on the side of my bed. "Stupid fucking Daemon called the paramedics," he mutters, almost to himself.

"Daemon?" I go to sit up, but it feels as though someone just launched a knife through my head. "Ahh." I reach up to rub it, and Bishop shoots toward me.

"Lie down. Don't try to act like a warrior. We all know you're tough; now just lie down."

The nurse walks in, putting her hands into her front pockets. "Hi, Madison, you're awake." She pulls out a little flashlight, hooking a stethoscope around her neck. Leaning forward, she smiles at both Bishop and me. "I'm just going to run a quick check before I give you more pain meds."

"No," Bishop interrupts. "Give her the meds now. The general practice bullshit you usually do will not fly in this room."

She goes to argue with Bishop, but then runs her eyes up and down his body, squaring her shoulders. "Very well."

She moves one of the drips around and turns the nozzle. "This is morphine. You will feel better soon. Can you tell me any other pain you are feeling aside from your head?"

"No," I murmur. "Just my head. It hurts really bad, almost unbearable, and I like to think I have a high pain threshold."

She smiles sweetly, but it doesn't reach her eyes. "Understandable. Your injury is severe."

"What is it, by the way?"

She looks to Bishop before looking back to me. "You were shot. Please, try to get some rest."

I was *shot?* Holy shit! How ironic is it that the one thing I love doing is the one thing that almost ended me... that ended my mom? Feeling tired, I close my eyes.

"Bishop?" she continues quietly.

My sleep can wait. Why does she know Bishop's name? I act like I'm unfazed anyway, keeping my eyes closed but kicking my hearing up a notch.

"These people have to leave."

"I know. But they're not going to."

People? What is she talking about?

"Well, it doesn't matter. They can't be sleeping on mattresses on the floor. Not only is it not sterile, but they're getting in the way."

"Jessica, leave."

"Bishop," she whispers, and I can almost feel the sadness in her tone.

"Leave!" he snaps at her.

Okay, I sense history there. I put that in the box of "will ask him one day." Once I hear the door close, I let my tiredness take over and drift into a deep sleep.

The next morning, I wake up almost instantly, and though I feel no better pain-wise, I feel a lot more alert than I did last night. I guess the Tillie thing is going to get ignored until I bring it up—and I will bring it up. I want to know why Bishop let her in. He must trust her to a certain extent. Usually, I would think maybe she has something to blackmail him with in some way, but this is Bishop. No one has anything on him, and if they did, he would just kill them.

Problem solved.

"Sis," Nate murmurs, getting off the mattress on the floor. Now I know what the little nurse was talking about last night. Nate and Tatum had obviously been sleeping out on the floor. Or more, wrapped around each other.

"Hi," I mutter, sitting up in my bed slightly. Bishop walks through the door, coffees and a bag of donuts in hand, just as Nate stands.

"Sorry, baby, you can't eat."

"What do you mean I can't eat?" I snap, my stomach growling on cue at the donuts he's holding.

"If they need to do emergency surgery, you have to be prepared, so you can't eat solids."

"Oh?" My eyebrow quirks. "Well guess who else isn't eating."

"What?" he growls.

"Drop them, Bishop."

"Fuck no! I'm hungry."

"Then you should have eaten them before you came back."

"I'm not dumping them."

I look at him.

"Fine, fuck. I'll leave them over here."

I look back to Nate. "Hi." He smiles, but his eyes are crinkled around the edges just like Bishop's. "Have you slept?" I look to Bishop. "Have any of you slept?"

They both shake their heads. Then Nate takes a seat on the bed. "We.... I need to tell you something."

"Okay?"

He grips my hand, his thumb caressing my palm slightly. "Daemon is currently locked up for questioning."

"What?" I go to shoot off the bed, but then wince when my head takes the beating.

As I lean back, Nate scolds me. "Do that shit again and I'll fucking kill you myself."

I roll my eyes, because only Nate can get away with threatening to kill me right after I almost got killed.

"But he didn't do anything!"

Nate searches my eyes. "You don't know that."

"Fuck you, I know that."

I see Bishop take a seat on one of the hospital chairs out the corner of my eye. Even from here, I can see how much he wants the donuts.

"Madison, you don't know Daemon. Yes, I know you guys are twins and I know you have that bond... but he's a very, very dangerous guy."

"Not to me." I look back at Nate. "I'm serious, Nate. He didn't do shit that day. He told me.... I remember, he told me to get back into the car and that something didn't feel right."

Nate doesn't flinch. Like he already knew I was going to say that. "Exactly, Madison. *He* knew something was going to happen."

"What does that mean?" I scoff, my anger reaching the boiling point. "You're not making sense."

"Fuck." Nate clutches his hair.

"Madi!" Tatum screams, launching off the mattress on the floor and diving onto my bed.

"Jesus fucking Christ, Tate!" Bishop jumps off his chair. "Get the fuck off her!" She climbs up my bed.

"I'm sorry! I'm sorry! It's just—" She bursts into tears, digging her head into my chest and curling up into a ball on top of me.

I pat her softly. "I know."

She swipes her tears angrily and slaps my arm. "Don't ever fucking do that again!"

"All right." Bishop wraps his arm around her waist and picks her up with one arm, removing her from my bed and putting her back down at the end. "Enough of that shit. I'm feeling unstable."

Tatum evil-eyes Bishop, brushing off her clothes snobbishly. "Don't you caveman me, Hayes!" Her eyes dart over his shoulder and her face lights up. "Oh!" She claps her hands and dives for the bag of donuts, pulling one out and biting into it. "Yum, donuts."

I can't help it; I laugh. Bishop gives me a dirty stare. "What? So she can eat a donut, but I can't?"

"Exactly."

He rolls his eyes and comes back up to my bed, sitting on the other side of me. I open my mouth, about to tell Nate to go on about Daemon, when the doors swing open and my dad and Elena walk in.

"Madison!" Elena wipes tears from her cheeks. "Oh, good Lord." She rushes near my bed and pulls me into a hug. I can hear Bishop growling beside me, the over-the-top male that he is.

"Hi," I whisper into her hair softly, looking up to my dad. His eyes are bloodshot red, wrinkles more prominent, and his suit looks a few days worn. "Hey, Dad."

Nate pulls his mother's arms off me. "All right, let her dad have a turn now. Ya stage five."

My dad leans down and kisses me on the head, leaving his kiss there for a beat longer. "I'm sorry, baby girl."

Closing my eyes, I exhale. All the stress and pain,

somehow he takes it all away. "It's not your fault, Dad."

He steps backward, his eyes searching mine. "You say that, Madison. But—"

I shake my head, and by God, it hurts to do so. "No. It is no one's fault."

His face changes, morphing into anger. "Madison," his voice turns into the firm one he uses whenever I'm in trouble, "you do not know anything about Daemon."

"How can you say that? He's your son!"

He opens his mouth and then closes it again. Looking over my shoulder to Bishop, he then looks back to me. "What do you want me to do?"

I smile. "Thank you. Get him the best lawyer. He will need it."

"I don't think this is—" Nate starts, but I cut him off.

"Shut up, Nate!" I look at Bishop. "Are you going to fight me on this too?"

He looks at me and then looks at my dad. "No. I got you, babe."

Those words. So simple, but meaning so much to me. My shoulders drop, and my heart slows for the first time since I've been here. "Thank you."

"I'll call around. I know one in New York. He's the best defense attorney in the state."

"Okay." I smile at my dad. "Thank you for doing this."

"For the record"—he looks at me, his eyebrows pulling in—"I'm not happy about it. There's a lot you have to learn. But I will respect your wishes enough to grant this for you. But if I find out that Daemon and his...." Dad pauses, then looks back at Bishop. "Never mind. Just—I'm doing this for you. No one else."

I nod. "Thanks, Dad."

"We better go. When can she come home?" he asks Bishop, and I don't miss the fact that Bishop takes charge of every situation. Even with my dad, who is decades older than him, it's still Bishop who runs shit. It's just Bishop. You don't get more… alpha? I don't know whether that's the right word to use, but he just commands everything. Like he's the alpha of a wolf pack, but the wolf pack is the human race in general. His tattoo is right; he pretty much is a god, and he doesn't even try. I don't know whether I want to kiss him or smack him. His ego doesn't need more feeding, so I'll go with a smack, and then kiss. Or a combination of both.

"She can leave today. She's been here for seven days because her heart skipped a couple beats after the incident. They said it was because of the trauma, her drifting in and out of consciousness was her body's way of dealing with it. The police want to ask her routine questions, too, and they have to because it's protocol. I'll be there the entire time, so no need to worry about that."

My dad straightens his tie that looks like it hasn't been knotted for at least a couple of days. "Thank you. I'll start on this phone call for Daemon, see if we can get the ball rolling faster."

Backpeddling, I just remember Bishop saying seven days, so when my dad and Elena leave, I turn to face him. "Seven days? I've been out for seven days?"

Bishop nods, walking toward Tatum and snatching the bag of donuts out of her hands before tossing them into the bin. "Yeah, but your injury is straight forward. You were grazed by the bullet, not actually shot." I guess that explains how I'm still alive and my throbbing headache.

Tatum snarls at him, leaning back in her chair. "Okay, so anyway." She looks to Bishop with her eyes large before smiling back to me. "Do you remember anything from that day, Mads?"

They all stop, Bishop and Nate both focusing in on me. I bite down on my lip, thinking over that afternoon. I remember it all. But do I tell them that? Or should I give them parts? I trust them, I do, but like Bishop and Nate have both said in the past, knowledge is power and secrets are weapons. Especially in this fucked up world.

I shrug her question off, picking at the old hospital blanket on my bed. "I mean, I remember some, not all. There's like, blank spots." I instantly feel awful for lying, but when I look at both her and Nate, I see they buy it. Until my eyes connect with Bishop, and instead of buying my lies, he sees straight through them. The slant in his evil glare gives that away.

Fuck.

Fuck Bishop and his ability to read people. Is there anything this fucker isn't good at? Because I've got nothing. I think I need to find what it is Bishop sucks at so I can attack it. Just for shits and giggles, and also because I know it'll drive him crazy. And I sort of like him when he's mad. That's a dangerous thing.

"Okay, well that's okay, right, Nate?" Tate looks to Nate, but he brushes her off, not giving her a second glance. She looks to the floor briefly, gathering her wits again after being shot down so easily. I see it. Right there, I see she's caught feelings for him.

"Agh," I moan lightly, annoyed at everything and everyone. "I just want to go home, to my bed, to my shower, to eat food, and watch Netflix in bed all night." I was meant to say that in my head, but I then realize I said it out loud.

Bishop chuckles. "Done. I'll go hurry the nurse. You will need to eat something solid before they let you leave though."

"Yeah, but I'm pretty sure Bishop runs the shots in this hospital too, so he will probably get you discharged anyway, what with all the pull he has. Must be nice being a king," Tatum adds sassily, one eyebrow raised to the high heavens. Ah, I see. That's why she's being extra salty toward Bishop; she knows, or has picked up on, or is just being Tatum—about something. Bishop is still glaring at her with his lip curled when he walks out the door. Silence doesn't last long once he's gone, because Tatum is instantly at my side.

"I saw Bishop with that nurse lady!" she whispers into my ear. Well, it was supposed to be a whisper, only Nate heard her from the other side of the room as he gathers up all his belongings.

"I heard that, and Tate? Leave it the fuck alone." Nate doesn't look at her or acknowledge her presence—at all. This would bother Tate, because as much as she keeps to herself at school, and as much as she's a loner, she's a loner by choice. Tatum is beautiful—drop-dead stunning. What with her lush blonde hair and rosy cheeks. She looks like a Victoria's Secret model. It's her attitude that needs fixing. But who am I to judge? That's probably why we get along so well.

"Why?" she snaps back at Nate.

He exhales, folding up the blanket and tossing it onto the chair. "Let's start with, it's none of your fucking business, and finish with, you'll just end up pissing off both our best friends." Nate stops, raising his eyebrows at her in challenge.

She squares up. "How about… your best friend is a piece

189

of shit, because while my best friend, AKA his…." She looks to me, and then looks to Nate, and then looks back to me again. "What are you two anyway?" she whispers.

I shrug. "Not something, but not nothing either."

Tatum's face drops. She's not impressed. "Madi, no, that's not a good place to be with a guy, because they have no rules and no boundaries. Men are simple creatures. They need lines. Simple lines."

"Well it works for us right now," I answer, pushing myself up off my bed. When she doesn't reply, I look at her. "Honestly, it really works for us right now. Whatever we have, it needs to be built slowly. We're too explosive. We wouldn't just blow each other up if this goes wrong; we'd take you all down with us."

Tatum mulls over what I've said and then walks back toward Nate. She spins around. "Okay, fine!"

"But…," I add.

Nate tosses the pillow on the other side of the room. "I knew it. I fucking knew this was coming."

"Fuck you," I snicker at him before looking back to Tatum. "What was it you saw?"

She searches my eyes then looks to Nate, and I brace myself. Brace myself for what everyone does when Nate, Bishop, or Brantley are in the room. It would probably happen if any of the other Kings were in the room too, but I just haven't been in the position. Tatum tilts her back as laughter erupts from her. Sarcastic laughter, but still laughter. She clutches her stomach, bringing her glare right back to Nate. "Naaw, Natey, I don't owe you or your pack of wolves shit. My loyalty is to Madison." She pauses and looks to me. "If I go missing, check their houses first." Then she slices to Nate. "She is my best friend, so fuck you and fuck Bishop."

"Fuck me?" Nate grins, and I fight the urge to massage my temples. "Well, you sure did, baby girl. Last night, in fact."

"Oh, gross, with me in the same room? Really?" I look at Tatum, because I expect more from her, though I really shouldn't.

She giggles. "My bad."

Rolling my eyes, I tilt my head up to the ceiling. "You were saying, Tate?" Bracing myself for the worst, while having an internal argument that whatever Bishop does is none of my business, Tatum opens her mouth.

"He had her up against the wall. He was... he...."

I don't need her to finish. I already know what she's going to say, and though I hate it, my heart sinks a little, and it's like sand has been siphoned down my airways every time I swallow. "He fucked her," I whisper through a clenched throat, swiping at the stray tear that has fallen down my cheek. Why do I care? I have no right to care. We're not together; we've never been official. This is probably why he didn't want us to go official, because he wanted to be a slut, and sluts don't like relationships.

But he's also told me things, things you shouldn't tell people unless you want them to grow feelings for you. My blood starts to boil a little before I start imagining what they were doing while I was in the hospital bed, what they—

"Madison!" Tatum snaps at me, clicking her fingers. "Jesus, Mary, and Joseph, girl! You really know how to zone out and get lost in that brain of yours." She has no idea. "As I was saying before you so rudely interrupted me"—she looks at me pointedly—"he had her up against the wall... by her throat."

I pause, blinking and catching what she's saying. So what? Bishop chokes me out during sex to the point of blacking out. What's her point?

She laughs, shaking her head. "No, you stupid cow. As in he was about to kill her."

Nate stills. "For the record, this is why we don't tell you anything. Remember this moment when you're throwing a tantrum about how you don't know anything." He tugs on his hoodie, zipping it up. Walking toward me, he presses a kiss to my head, hooking his finger under my chin to tilt my face up to his. "I'll go get the house ready for you, okay?"

I nod. "Thanks, Nate."

"Anytime." He smiles at me softly before glaring at Tatum. "Shut your mouth, Tate. Watch what you say if you like breathing."

She rolls her eyes and sits on the bed. Once Nate is out of the room, I look toward Tatum. I can see she's a little upset about the way Nate has been acting all morning. "For the record," I note, "I totally said you and Nate sleeping together would be a bad idea."

She opens her mouth, ready to defend herself, when she exhales in defeat. "Girl, you have no idea."

Actually, I do.

The door opens again, and Bishop walks in with the nurse from earlier scurrying not far behind him. "Usually the doctor would need to discharge you, but he's left it to me. You will need to eat something and sign paperwork at reception on your way out." She smiles, but it's strained, not reaching her eyes. She's just about to say something when another nurse walks in, pushing a cart full of food.

"Thanks," I murmur. I hate hospital food, but I can

stomach a sandwich. Especially if it gets me out of here.

I take a bite, finishing it in record time before looking back to the nurse. "Thank you." I nod then gaze to Bishop, who's staring at me with his jaw clenched. Great. What the hell have I done now?

"Where'd Nate go?" Bishop finally breaks the awkward silence as the nurse starts removing my IV drips.

I wince slightly. "Home to get my room ready or something."

Bishop smiles and then looks to Tatum. "You didn't want to go with him?"

Tatum narrows her eyes on him. "Why would I want to do that?"

"Because you're you."

The drive home was painful. Between Bishop and Tatum both making a fuss over everything, I was almost ready to jump out of a moving vehicle on the freeway and walk home. And if I did, I would have survived, because for the first time ever, Bishop was going 10 mph, not wanting to go over potholes and bumps in the road.

Walking up the stairs, I push open my bedroom door, annoyed at both of them and wanting some space, but when I walk in, I gasp. "What the…?"

Nate sits on a mattress at the foot of my bed and has spread out the entire surface with cheesecakes, gummy bears, and my favorite chocolate, Debauve & Gallais's Le Livre.

There are sushi rolls lined in a circle platter with soy dipping sauce in the middle. Next to it is a round of tacos, and all the dipping sauces for fries and potato skins.

"Nate!" I smile. If I wasn't so sore, I'd jump his bones.

"Hey, Kitty." He grins, and because he's Nate, he looks all seductive. Or maybe I'm turned on by the food. "You hungry?" He wiggles his eyebrows and flexes his pecs.

I roll my eyes. "Yes, my God."

"Wow, Riverside, you sure know how to put on a show," Tatum mutters, walking into the room and grabbing her bag. She looks at me. "I'm going to go home, sleep for a hundred days in my own bed, and not talk to anyone for at least a month. She smiles, walking up to me and pulling me in for a hug. "I'll text you, okay?"

Nodding, I smile. "You better." Then she turns and exits, leaving me to deal with both Nate and Bishop.

"Actually," Nate smiles, getting off the mattress and dusting off his pants, "I didn't do any of this. Bishop did." He leans down, stealing a taco and shoving it into his mouth.

"So you just took it? No correcting me or Tatum?" I arch my eyebrow.

He shakes his head, swallowing his food. "She's fun to play with. That's all."

I unzip my hoodie and toss it onto my bed. "Don't hurt her, Nate."

"Hey!" He throws his empty hands up. "She knows where I stand. It's not my fault if she catches feelings. She's good in bed. That's all I want."

"What? And fuck around on her in the meantime?" I ask, reaching up and touching the gauze that's wrapped around my head.

He watches me and then cusses under his breath. "None of that matters. We aren't a thing. There's only one—or maybe two girls who had the power to change that, and one of them was you. Anyway, you feeling okay? You need anything?"

He looks to Bishop, who is sprawled out on my bed, shirt-less with gray sweatpants on and the rim of his Calvin Klein briefs poking out the top.

I'm screwed.

"I'm sure B will take care of you, right?"

Bishop reaches forward on my bed and grabs the remote, flicking the TV on. "Go to bed, Nate."

Nate winks at both of us before walking back through to his room. Bishop must push Play on a movie because it cuts through our silence. But it's not an awkward silence or the kind of silence you feel when you're in a room with someone you're uncomfortable with.

"I'm just going to take a shower," I say to him, walking to my closet to get a pair of sweatpants and a tank top.

He nods, watching as I pass him. Once I've gathered ev-erything I need, I flick the light off and start walking back toward the bathroom, only Bishop catches my hand as I pass him, his fingers caressing my palm.

I turn to look at him over my shoulder. "You okay?" He's not usually touchy-feely, so this is new territory we're both walking through, but it feels right. He makes my heart race and my blood rush, but it feels right.

Tilting his head, he looks into my eyes then runs his thumb over my knuckles. "Yeah, yeah, I am now. Want me to run you a bath? You don't want to get that wet." He points up to my head, and I touch it, remembering the bandage and remembering I got shot—or grazed.

But still, I got shot.

Oh my God.

"What's wrong?" he asks, obviously noticing my facial expressions. Tilting his head to the other side, his fingers stay laced with mine.

I grin a little. "I'm a bit of a badass. I've been shot!"

He chuckles, letting go of my hand and slapping my ass. "Get in the shower."

I bite down on my lip and quickly rush into the bathroom.

"And lock that fucking door!" Bishop yells, his voice vibrating through the thin walls.

I laugh, shaking my head and unbuttoning my jeans before slipping them off. Scrubbing myself in the shower, I want to stay in for longer than I do but I also really want to be near Bishop right now, so I flick off the faucet and grab the towel, wrapping it around myself. Drying my body, I already feel much better than I did five minutes ago. Slipping on my boyshorts and my loose gray sweatpants, I toss on my tight black tank and put my towel in the hamper before pulling open my bedroom door. Leaning on the doorframe, I smile at Bishop, who's biting into one of the sushi rolls.

"Good?"

"Not bad, but I guess it will taste even better to you because you haven't eaten in so long." I push off the wall and make my way toward him, taking a seat beside him on the mattress. Grabbing a taco, I dip it into the guacamole and bite into the crispy shell.

"Mmmmm," I groan, unable to help the pleasure that takes over my body as my taste buds get their first taste of the taco.

Bishop pauses, sushi roll midway to his mouth. "Don't do that."

"Do what?" I ask innocently, licking the sauce off my fingers.

He drops the sushi roll back onto the platter. "Madison...."

I roll my eyes. "I won't do that, but! Only because I'm starving and I actually feel like I'm about to eat every single thing on this platter."

"Good." He grins, picking up the sushi roll and popping it back into his mouth.

I chow down my taco, not making a single sound. Reaching for my water bottle, I twist it open, swallowing the cool liquid.

"So tell me, how'd you know all of this was my favorite food?" I ask Bishop, stretching out on the mattress because my stomach feels like it's about to explode. Looking up at the ceiling, I eventually look toward him when he doesn't say anything.

"I know all there is to know about you, Madison." He moves the platter to the other side of the mattress and slides beside me. "Ask me anything."

"Hmmm." I bring my finger to my lip, pretending to mull over some questions. "Okay, how about this?"

Bishop raises his eyebrows cockily.

"Where was I born?"

"New York, try harder than that."

He's right; that was too easy. "My first pet's name?"

"Billy and he was a goldfish. You were seven and de-manded your mom buy it for you so you'd have a friend, be-cause you were an only child. Furthermore, you used that same excuse for Jasper the Persian cat, Slash—by the way, nice choice of name—the Pomeranian—not a fan of giving such a powerful name to such a tiny dog either—and Jupiter, your parrot." He tilts his head, egging me to challenge him.

I don't. I just stare, because what else could I do? Nothing surprises me much in this world now since finding out about the Kings, but it's still a lot to take in.

"Wow," I whisper out, rolling onto my stomach. I lean my head on the palm of my head and look up at him. He's sitting up with his back leaning against the bedframe, but his legs are spread out in front of him.

"You have me at a disadvantage then," I whisper, locking eyes with him. "I don't know much about you."

He snorts, leaning back, his ab muscles tensing as he does it. "Don't take it to heart. No one knows anything about me." He closes his eyes and reaches out. "Come here." Two simple words but so commanding. I don't fight it. I scoot up the mattress and snuggle into his warm, hard arms. His familiar scent starts to smell more like home and less like Bishop. Running the tip of my nose against his chest, I draw lines across his pec, over the tattoo that is inked into his skin. It's an eagle, soaring freely. "This is cool." I yawn.

He grunts. "Yeah, but I bet you could draw something better."

That makes me smile. "I could."

My eyes drop heavily, and I can slowly feel myself slipping into sleep.

"Will you draw one for me one day?" he asks in a tired voice. The sexiest sleepy voice I've ever heard. I sound like a man when I'm tired, so I clear my throat.

"Yes."

He squeezes me into him softly, and just like that, I slip into a deep sleep.

Cool air drifts over my legs, goose bumps breaking out over my skin. I reach over blindly to grab the blanket when Bishop tosses and turns. "No!" he yells. I shoot up and look at him. Sweat is dripping over his skin, his arm thrown over his eyes. He starts punching his head. "No! Leave him alone. Leave her alone!"

"Bishop!" I grab onto his arm, wanting to stop his assault on himself. "Bishop? Shhhh…." Lava builds in my throat as tears threaten to surface. What's he dreaming about?

"Bishop?"

"No! Leave him alone, leave him alone, leave her alone…!"

Rolling over, I straddle his waist, clearing the sweat from his chest. "Hey," I whisper, leaning into his ear. "It's me."

His jaw clenches before he finally opens his eyes and looks straight at me.

"Hey," I repeat, running my fingers down his cheeks and swiping away the sweat. "You okay?"

He stares at me, unmoving. It starts to get awkward, so I swing my leg off him but he clenches down on my thigh. I look back at him. "Bi—"

His fist comes to my hair and he wraps it around, pulling my face down to meet his.

"Well," I mutter under my breath. "Good thing my graze in on my temple."

I don't say another word. I go with it. Something has happened, something inside his head, so I'll do what I can to help. Kissing me, his tongue slips between my lips. I open my mouth wider, giving him more access. Gripping onto my thighs, he flips me onto my back and spreads my legs wide with his, pinning my arms above my head.

His eyes skim over the side of my head. "Are you good to go?" I know what he's asking. He's asking if I'm ready to fuck—fuck Bishop style.

"Yes," I answer truthfully, because I am. Aside from a little headache, nothing else hurts, and if it does, whatever, I'll pay for it in the morning, and I'm sure it'll be worth it.

"Fuck," he growls, his voice unrecognizable.

Looking over his face, his eyes slam closed as he pulls his bottom lip into his mouth. "Yes, Bishop," I repeat softly. "I promise—no limits. I can take it. I can handle it." I'll probably regret that,

I reach out to swipe the bead of sweat that's about to drip off his chin, but he hits my hand away. "Don't."

"What?" I murmur.

"Not now."

He pins my hands above my head, his palms gliding up my thighs until he gets to the waistband of my sweatpants then tugs them off. His fingertips glide over the lining of my underwear before slipping underneath to press inside me.

"Get up."

"What?" I whisper, confused. He gets to his knees just as "Escalate" by Tsar B starts blasting from Nate's room. The song has a heavy bass line, and it sounds so clear that it's as if it's playing in here.

Bishop pulls down his jeans, getting to his feet at the side of the bed and tossing off his boxer briefs. I stare down at his cock and watch as he slowly pumps it, his eyes locked on mine. Grinning, he nudges his head. "Get up, baby."

Crawling, I tilt my head. "But why?"

"Because you're going to do what I say."

"Bu—"

His hand flies up to my neck, and he instantly squeezes, tugging my head up to look at him. His shoulders are square, his stance stiff, strong, and thick like always. This is Bishop, and always will be Bishop. He's alpha out there; he has to be because of who he is. But in the bedroom, his alpha tendencies have no bounds. The song must be on repeat because it plays again.

I close my eyes, nodding. "What do you want me to do?"

His grip loosens and he steps backward, grabbing his pack of cigarettes off the chest of drawers, the moonlight sneaking through the cracks of my patio door, outlining him perfectly. His face, his profile, that body, that… dick. He's perfection wrapped in a case of C4. He puts a cigarette between his lips, flicks his Zippo, and looks at me after lighting it, a grin on his face. Sucking on his cigarette, he tilts his head back to blow out the smoke, his neck straining at the movement. I look down at his hand, still holding his dick, slowly pumping it, and my mouth waters. Holy shit. I've never seen something so erotic in my life. Sweat beads on my flesh as my clit throbs between my thighs. I want him.

Fuck. I want him. The way my nipples feel, as though they're getting whisked with the breeze, and the way my hips start rolling to the rhythm of his pumping, tells him how badly. He chuckles, leaving the cigarette between his lips, and walks toward me. His legs hit the side of the bed, and he takes the smoke out of his mouth.

I look up at him, my hands running up his muscular thighs. Pulling in my bottom lip, I run my tongue over it and reach for his cock.

Blowing out a cloud of smoke, he looks down at me, our eyes entranced in each other. Locked in a cell that's sealed with lust. "Suck." His lip curls slightly, the grin still on his face and his smoke between his thumb and pointer finger.

I look down to the tip of him, licking my lips again, and

lean forward, wrapping my mouth around him securely. His precum hits the back of my throat, and I moan slightly, my tongue dancing up his long length. He grips onto my hair, piling it all on the top of my head then tugs on it, yanking my head backward. Again, I'm thanking whoever it was that saved me that day for the bullet skimming the side of my temple, and not anywhere near where any hair pulling happens.

I look up at him, my lips wrapped around him while my head bobs. He sucks on the last bit of his smoke, then turns toward the porch door and flicks it out before turning back to me and shoving me onto the bed. "Lay down."

"Like I have a choice." I roll my eyes.

He pins my hands above my head, spreading my legs wide open with his, and runs his nose down the side of my neck. "Mmm," he groans, and it vibrates over my flesh before sinking into my bones. I quiver, goose bumps rolling over my skin. His grin presses against my flesh before I feel his tongue slide down my collarbone then down over my nipple. Pulling it into his mouth, he bites down roughly, and I wince.

"Bishop," I warn, remembering how rough he can get.

"Not your place to say, Kitty. Remember that."

"Safe word."

"And I said fuck your safe word." As he circles my nipple with his tongue, my eyes close and my hips rise to grind against his, needing more. More friction. Needing him inside of me, filling me until I can barely take the pain of his size.

"How will you know if it's too far for me?" I ask, circling my pelvis into him. He raises slightly, not letting me gain any more friction or pleasure, and I have to fight just putting my hand down there and taking care of the ache myself.

He continues his travels, leaving a warm trail of goose

bumps in his wake. "Guess if you die, that's a sign."

My eyes snap open and I lean up on my elbows. "Bishop!"

He peers up at me, hovering just over my pelvic bone, his arms rippling from holding himself up. He grins, his eyes darkening. "I'm just joking." His tongue comes out and licks over my clit. "I think." Letting go, I drop onto my back, my hair sprawling out everywhere. He grips onto my thigh and pushes me open wider, while his other arm hooks my thigh over his shoulder. He licks me at a perfect rhythm, never stopping, never changing. Never too fast and never too slow. Just as my stomach clenches and sweat trickles over my abs, I'm grasping onto the edge of sanity, about to fall off into my orgasm, when he stops. Everything turns cold, my entire body dropping to an icy temperature instantly.

"Agh!" I scream, getting onto my elbows. He crawls up my body, licking his lips while his eyes fuck every inch of me.

"Mine." His hand comes to mine and he flings them over my head again, pinning me down. "Don't fuck with me, Madison. You're mine." He squeezes roughly, rough enough to leave marks on my wrists, and I flinch. He smirks and then releases, flinging me onto my stomach, he rubs my ass cheek softly before whacking it hard, the loud slap breaking through the song I can still hear. Moving my hair to one side, he grabs onto my thigh and hooks it onto his hip before I feel his weight fall over my back and his cock press at my entrance.

I moan at the sudden intrusion, and his other hand comes up to the back of my neck, pressing me into place as he sinks farther and farther into me, pushing every single limit I have. Gripping onto my thigh, the tips of his fingers dig into my flesh as he pulls out of me, thrusting over my G-spot every single time and then launching into me again, my body almost flying forward. His grip on the back of my neck tightens and then loosens as he brings his body back over mine while still gripping my thigh up against his hip. He thrusts into me, circling and rubbing me deep. My pussy clenches around him, clinging on and not letting go. Every extraction, I clench harder. Lost in the way his cock presses against every single inch of my core. Owning me from the inside out.

"Yes," I moan. "Bishop, fuck me."

He lets go of my leg, pulls out, flips me over, and picks me up, rolling onto his back. I climb on top of him, slowly dropping my weight over his hard dick. Leaning on his chest, I roll my hips, his cock thrusting inside me as his pelvic bone collides with my clit. I swing my head back, and his hips buckle as he clenches onto mine.

"Come."

As if on cue, I let go, sweat dripping off both our bodies. I clench around him, throbbing as the orgasm smashes through me and I jerk through the ecstasy.

"Fuck!" His hips slam up, pushing my body up faster and harder, plowing through my orgasm to reach his. He sets me off again, and wave after a wave, another orgasm collides into me, my clit swelling, my nipples cool. Bishop leans up, catches one of my nipples in between his teeth, and bites down on it. It stings, but the sting with the pleasure is too much. His hand comes up to my throat while his other stays on my hip and he lies back down, a touch of blood on the corner of his lip. I don't have to look to know where that's from; the stinging of my nipple says enough.

His fingers dig into my hips, his grip around my throat tightening to the point where air is coming in and out slowly, like I'm breathing through a thick cloud of smoke. He pounds into me, his balls slapping against my ass as I try to regain control being on top of him, but there's no point. He is always in control no matter what, so I let go. Dots dance in my eyes from being choked, my thighs throb from his grip, and now my hips are stinging too. He slams into me harder, and I feel it again, the build-up. My head swings back. I'm exhausted, but I'm not able to stop the pleasure. He's fucking the life out of me, quite literally, because I can feel myself losing consciousness every now and then, but I notice how he loosens his grip every few seconds too, as if to give me little cracks of air.

I'm just about to hit the tip of my orgasm when he comes, his dick throbbing and pulsing inside of me. He lets go of me instantly, and I ride it out with him slowly. I wanted another, but I know I'm being greedy, and I can already feel how sore I am, not only everywhere where he's physically hurt me, but down there too. Wincing, I swing my leg and get off, feeling his cum drip down my thigh.

"I get the depo shot," I say sleepily, dragging my sore and severely fucked self to the bathroom and pulling down a towel to clean myself up. He still hasn't said anything, so I look at him. "Are you okay?"

"Yeah," he answers through a dry throat. Getting up, he tugs on his boxers and walks toward the little bar fridge I have in the room. Surprisingly, even though I just had rough sex, my head doesn't feel bad. Or I'm just that sore everywhere else on my body that my pain threshold has sort of tilted this way.

Bishop gets a bottle of water and twists off the cap, taking a drink while looking at me.

"Wanna talk about it?" I ask, throwing the towel into a hamper and going back to bed. Fuck the rumpled blankets; I can't even be bothered remaking my bed, so I just slip under, sliding onto the side I sleep on. When Bishop doesn't answer, I look over to the little alarm clock that sits on my bedside table. Fucking 5:00 a.m.? Mother fuck.

"It's 5:00 a.m.!" I yell, honest to God shocked at the time.

"Then we fucked for three hours."

"How do you know that?" I ask, watching as he slips back into bed with me.

He stretches his arms out, pulling me into him. I don't know why, but I smile, my heart calming at his touch, his smell, his flesh pressing against mine. All those things are why Bishop is home to me.

He kisses me on my head. "Because the terrors happen at the same time every night."

"Why?" I whisper, yawning and beginning to feel more and more pain all over my body. I'll hate to see what I'm going to look like later in the morning.

"Because I've done bad things. And those bad things like to remind me every night that I did them."

I swallow, my eyes heavy even though my interest in this convo is piquing. My body and mind can't keep up. "Did what?"

"Killed and fucked."

CHAPTER 21

I can't move. That's not a figure of speech. I literally cannot move a muscle in my body, and I'm not sure if I should be genuinely concerned about this or not.

"Bishop?" I croak. Gross, I hate my morning voice. I sound like a man that's been lost in the desert for years.

His arm is clenched around my waist, pulling me into him while his leg is over mine. So not only am I in pain and can't move, but his heavy-ass weight is holding me down too. Surprise, surprise, he's even possessive in his sleep.

"Bishop!" I get a little louder, trying to pry his limbs off mine.

"What?" he groans, letting me go and rubbing his eyes.

I go to move my leg and… nope, that's not happening. "Nothing. I just… I can't move," I laugh, shaking my head.

He stops rubbing his eyes and looks at me, and fuck him.

His ruffled hair is messy everywhere, his dark green eyes fresh, his skin pure, and his lips kissable and plump.

"I think," I murmur, tilting my head at him. "Nope, not think—I definitely want to punch you."

He bursts out laughing. "Well—" Lifting the blanket, he scans over my naked body. "I don't think that's a good idea, babe. I mean… you're in a state right now."

He drops the blanket, and I pick it back up and peer down at myself.

"Oh my God!" I gasp in shock and then narrow my eyes at Bishop. "Are you kidding me? I look like I've been beaten."

"Hey!" He throws his hands up. "You know how I get, and I'm pretty sure I went a little easy on you."

"Oh really?" I scold him, flicking the blanket off my body and walking toward the bathroom. "'Cause I'm pretty sure that's my blood on your fucking lip!" I slam the door closed and then bite down on my fist, holding in my scream. My whole body throbs. My hips, my thighs…. My neck feels like there's a massive ring still clenched around it, and my freaking nipple feels like it's been torn off, and to make everything worse, my vagina feels fucking swollen, because oh no, he can't just mark me in one place; he has to absolutely destroy me. Flicking on the faucet, I slowly step into the hot, steamy water, and I scream before I can stop myself. "Motherfucker!"

Nate bangs on his door, because I locked it. "Mads! What's wrong?"

"Leave me alone," I yell out. "Pretty sure you knew what was happening too, motherfucker," I mutter under my breath, grabbing the soap and sliding it through my hands. Now that the initial sting is gone from stepping in, the water pounding on my bruised flesh is actually comforting.

Bang.

Bang.

"Madison!" Nate calls again through the door. I roll my eyes and flip him the bird, grabbing my towel and wrapping it around myself. "What?"

"Are you okay?"

"I'm hungry. I'm going to get something to eat."

"I'll do it. Go back to bed!"

"Don't—"

"Madison," he growls.

"I want to see Daemon. Shut up and stop telling me what to do!" I go to grab my clothes when I realize I didn't bring any in with me. Fuck.

I walk out, but Bishop is gone. Looking around my room suspiciously, I check the closet, coming up short. Staying in the closet, I wiggle into some white skinny jeans, a black top, and some sneakers before grabbing a sweater. I remember the nurse saying I can remove the Band-Aid today, so I unwrap that from my head, feeling the coolness whipping over my newly exposed skin. There's still a couple of butterfly stitches where my wound is, so I leave it there. The wound itself doesn't hurt anymore; it's just the light headache that throbs in the back of brain that does. Then again, that could be from Bishop's hair pulling the night before. Though I know that he could have been a lot rougher with the pulling than he was.

I toss the Band-Aid into the trash and grab my keys. I don't care what either of them say; I want to see my brother. He didn't do anything wrong. I just know he didn't.

I was wrong about one thing, though. I definitely regret nothing about last night.

Walking into the local police station, I go straight to the front reception desk. "Hi." The receptionist looks up at me from her typing, pushing her glasses down. She's old, and by the looks of the scowl she's giving me, she's not having a good day. "I was wondering how I go about seeing my brother? He was brought in a few days ago after an incident."

She stops me with a simple whip of her hand. "Daemon—"

"Madison?" My dad's voice breaks through from behind me. "What are you doing here?"

I turn to face him, plastering a fake smile on my face. "Oh! Hey, Dad!"

I look back to the receptionist, where she looks at me with an eyebrow quirked, eyeing me up and down. Looking back to my dad, I walk up to him. "I was just wondering if I could see Daemon."

Dad looks at me suspiciously. "He's out on bail. Happened just this morning. I take it he will be at home now."

I can't help the smile that comes onto my mouth, my chest warming. "At our home? Okay, I'll go up there now."

"Madison." My dad puts his hands into his pockets. "We need to talk about Daemon though, so I'll get Sammy to meet us back at home."

"Okay," I whisper, relaxing so much more, now that I know he's on bail and at home. I can't imagine Daemon in a prison cell, and he doesn't deserve to be in one. I know what people say about him, but he would never hurt me—regardless of what he does or has done to other people. I don't know why I have such certainty about Daemon, but I do. My ease with him is effortless. Maybe it's a twin thing, I don't know.

I follow Dad back out of the station and wait as he tells

Sammy that she can meet us back at home.

"So," I begin, unlocking the truck and getting into the driver side. Dad gets into the passenger seat and clips in his belt. "What is it you want to talk about?"

"Daemon."

"Yes, we can start with him," I murmur, pulling out into the oncoming traffic. "Why?"

Dad looks at me. I can see him from the corner of my eye. "Why what?"

"Why didn't you and Mom want him?" I ask, risking a quick glance toward him. "I mean, it just doesn't seem fair that I got this life and he got his."

"Whose life do you think is worst?"

Interesting question, but that's Dad for you. He has always had a way of expressing his knowledge—a way I hated growing up.

"I don't know," I scoff. "Don't make me answer that. I got a luxurious life, though it hasn't been easy at times, and I've…." I clear my throat, not wanting to get too touchy with this subject. "But Daemon's life seems messed up, Dad. So why? Why'd you and Mom decide he wasn't worthy of your love?"

"It's not that, Madison. He wasn't fit to be a King, so he had to be a Lost Boy."

I laugh. I can't help it, but "he's not fit to be a King" just grinds me the wrong way. "That makes no sense."

"You will never make sense of this world. You need to understand that." He looks at me, and I glance back at him. "Trying to figure out this world will never happen, Madison, and it will kill you like it has killed many others who tried."

Taking my eyes off him, I look back to the road. "There

are so many questions."

Dad nods. "Yes," he looks ahead of himself, "and just when you think you know everything, something else gets thrown into the mix," he mutters under his breath, almost like he didn't mean for me to hear.

"Like what, Dad?"

He looks back to me and smiles, the wrinkles around his eyes deepening. "That's not for you to worry about. Just be careful with Daemon. I know he wouldn't… intentionally hurt you. But he's a dangerous sort, Madison. He's so very dangerous."

"Why do people keep saying that?" I don't mean to, but it comes out as if I'm annoyed. I guess I am. I've seen a glimpse into the dark side of Daemon. I say glimpse because of the way people are talking about him makes it seem like he has a very, very dark part about him. But even in that mode, he wouldn't hurt me.

"Because it's the truth." Dad exhales. "Just be careful. If I tried to explain Daemon to you, it still wouldn't scratch the surface, but I have rules."

"Rules?" I inch my head back. "Since when do you give me rules?"

"Since a bullet grazed your temple, Madison!" He raises his voice a little toward the end but then breathes out, exhaling all his anger. "Look, stick to these rules or I will father you, and I don't care how old you are."

"Fine." I slump into my chair, pulling down our street. "What are your rules?"

"You are not to be alone with Daemon under any circumstances. The Kings know, so if you want to spend time with him, one of them needs to be there with you."

"That's bullshit!"

"No, that's the rule. They don't have to be right beside you, but they need to be there." I pull into our gated driveway. "Elena and I are flying to Dubai tomorrow morning. Stick to that one rule or I will be on the first flight home, understood?" He looks at me just as I pull up the emergency brake.

"Fine."

"Good." Dad smiles. "Oh, I've moved Daemon to the bedroom on the other side of Nate's room."

"Why?" I ask, getting out of the truck and rounding to the front. "Why not beside my room?"

Dad stops, tilting his head at me. "Does it matter?"

I open my mouth, ready to answer, but close it again. "I guess not." Because it doesn't. At least he's here, and Dad is allowing him to stay. I have to be grateful for that, though Katsia will want that meeting ASAP. I can't stand her and I don't trust her. She's apparently a descendant of Bishop's family line, and though I've only met Bishop's dad a couple of times, I don't like him. He's the king of the Kings, and there's no way in hell I'd ever cross him. Same as Katsia.

Taking the stairs one at a time, I go straight to Daemon's room and knock.

"Come in."

Pushing the door open, I lean on the frame. "Hey, you."

He smiles, a genuine, big smile, and his eyes light up. He gets up off the bed where he was sitting oddly, staring at.... There's no TV there, so he was staring at the wall. As he pulls me in for a hug, I wrap my arms around his waist and sink into his embrace. "I'm so sorry about all of this, Daemon."

"Hush," he murmurs into my hair. "They just like you safe. Like me. I like that too."

"Yeah, but they should trust that I trust you."

Daemon inches back slightly, his eyebrows pulling in as he seems to mull over what I just said. "Trust," he whispers, and then looks down at me.

"Yes, trust. It's the feeling you get when you know someone won't hurt you. It's loving someone and knowing they wouldn't betray you."

Daemon shakes his head, and lets go, stepping backward. "No, Madison. If that is trust, I do not deserve yours. You should not trust me."

I step forward. "Daemon, I do though."

He shakes his head, stepping back again until the backs of his legs hit the rocking chair that is in the corner. He takes a seat. "No. You cannot."

"Daemon—"

"Madison," Bishop speaks up from the door, and I turn to face him, searching his eyes.

"What?"

"Leave. Now."

"What?" I snap, then look back to Daemon. "Do you want me to leave?"

Daemon looks up at me from leaning on his elbows, his eyes pained and his face strained. It's the first time I've seen him in any other light aside from my brother, and he's beautiful. Beautifully ruined. "*Ita.*"

I look back to Bishop, not knowing what that means. He simply nods, so I look back at Daemon. "Okay."

I push past Bishop and walk toward my bedroom, flopping down on my bed. Seconds and then minutes pass before Bishop walks back in, shutting the door behind him.

I shoot to my feet. "Is he okay?"

He walks farther into my room, taking a seat on the bed beside me. "Yeah. When he's like that though, Madison, you need to let him have space. Nothing good will come from pushing Daemon to a point where…." He stops, seeming to think over what he's about to say.

"Bishop," I warn, looking toward him. "You need to not lie to me." He lies down on his back, and I follow, rolling onto my stomach. "Please. Just don't lie to me. I can handle everyone else lying to me, but not you."

Turning his head, he looks between my eyes. It's intense. His stare is always intense; it makes me want to look away, but I'm afraid I won't feel it again. I want to feel it for as long as I can. Soak it up, bathe in it, swim in it. Now I sound crazy, but maybe I am. Maybe when it comes to him, he brings out the dark, crazy side of me that I've always suppressed by being the quiet girl. Because he gives me confidence, all the confidence I need to tackle or do anything, and that's lethal.

Reaching out, he tucks some of my loose hair behind my ear and smiles softly. "I promise I won't lie to you."

I inhale, unable to contain the warm feeling that overflows my insides at his promise. Not once has anyone—not my father, not Nate, no one—promised me those words since I've found out about this world. Leaning down, I kiss him, running my lips softly against his. I'm just about to pull away when his hand comes to the back of my neck and he grips onto me, pulling me back down to his mouth. His tongue darts inside and everything in me instantly comes to life. Picking me up, he puts me on his lap, and I straddle him, raking my hair out of my face.

"I'm not used to this," he murmurs, his hands coming to rest on my thighs.

"Used to what?" I ask, running my pointer finger down his hard chest, over each ab muscle, and eventually down to the lines that disappear under his jeans.

"This, what this is. I'll fuck it up one way or another. You're prepared for that—right?" he asks, his tone sincere.

I shrug, looking back into his eyes. "I guess we can cross that bridge when we get there." I open my mouth, wondering whether or not I should ask the question that is itching at the back of my brain. "Khales?" I must have decided I was going to go there, because before I can stop myself, I say it.

His jaw tenses. "It's not as you or everyone thinks." He taps me, and I swing my leg off him, scooting up the bed and leaning on the headboard.

"So tell me then. What was she?"

"A close friend. We were always together, because she was a friend. You know your Tatum? The girl you met before you knew about the Kings?"

I nod, slightly nervous at where this conversation could go. It's the first time Bishop has ever opened up about Khales, and I don't want to say something dumb and have him clam up again. "Yeah, but haven't you boys always known about the Kings?"

He laughs, running his hands through his hair and leaning on his elbows, his back turned toward me. "No. It's not until you're of age when you're given the book. I had known Khales since we were in preschool."

"Who was she?" I ask, tilting my head. "I know she went to Tillie's school and all that."

"Yeah." He clears his throat. "She had a shitty life, and then eventually started playing with drugs. I always tried to help her where I could, but sometimes you can't help those who don't want to be helped. Anyway, she kicked the drugs, and after I was initiated, she and I got close again. That is until my father decided otherwise."

"Initiated? You mean after you…?"

He looks at me over his shoulder then turns to face me fully, leaning back on one of the posts at the end of my bed. "I'm sure you know about the initiation process."

I blush. "Yes… how old?"

"Thirteen." He looks at me carefully. "I'm sure you know what happens after…."

"Your first kill?" I ask lightly. I already know the answer, so I pull my eyes away from his and look at the wall.

"Truth?" he replies gently.

My eyes snap back to him. "Always."

"Then, no, it wasn't my first kill."

I breathe in deeply. "Well, okay."

"Okay?" He chuckles, shaking his head and pulling his bottom lip between his teeth. "I tell you that I killed someone when I was younger than thirteen, and you say 'okay?' Like it's the most natural thing in the world?" He looks back at me, a mixture of awe and anger in his stare.

"Well," I reply, "in our world, it is natural."

"True," he agrees.

"So your dad? He made you kill her?" I want to tread carefully around her, and I probably should have found a better word than kill, but I need straightforward answers, and to get straight answers, you need to ask straightforward questions. Leave them no gap to dance around their answer.

His jaw clenches. "Something like that." I can see it's a touchy subject, and aside from the fact that Bishop isn't someone who opens up, I don't want to push it. I don't want to use the fact he just promised me he wouldn't lie to bleed answers out of him.

Smiling, I shake my head. "Hungry?"

He snaps up at me in shock, "What? You're not going to push for more answers?"

I shrug, getting off the bed. "No, I figure if I go in too hard, you might clam up, and I really am hungry." My phone dings in my pocket and I pull it out, opening the text from Tatum.

Tate - You home?
Me - Yep.
Tate - I'll come up soon.

Tossing my phone back on the bed, Bishop looks at it then back to me. "It was Tate," I answer his unspoken question. "She'll come up soon."

He laughs, getting off the bed and stretching his arms high. "I figured."

The following few days have gone better than I expected. Aside from Daemon's lawyer building his case, Bishop and I have fallen into a smooth... relationship? I'm actually not sure what we are, and I don't want to interrupt the flow of things by asking for a label. Daemon hasn't left his room though, and that worries me. Everyone I have expressed my angst to about him not leaving his room has told me to leave it alone and that he's dealing with things the way he knows how. So out of respect for Daemon, I do just that. I've left it.

"I need to ask you something," Tate says, peeling off the lid of her yogurt. "Please don't get mad at me for bringing it up, but it's been itching at me for some time."

Biting into my apple, I roll my hand for her to continue—at least until the boys get here, and then I'm sure she will tense up like she always does. I'm not sure what is going on with her and Nate, but I've decided to leave that too, not wanting to go near their drama.

"Okay, so the tape…," she starts, and I pause my chewing, looking around the cafeteria in panic mode.

"Tatum!" I snap at her through a whisper. "Why would you bring that up?" I sit straight, biting into my apple again.

"Well, I don't know. Maybe because you haven't mentioned it."

"Well I just want to forget." I give her a pointed stare.

"I just have this thing. So who sent it? Ally?" She won't stop. Someone needs to gag her.

"Apparently so—yes."

"But here's the thing." She spoons her yogurt into her mouth. "Ally was apparently at a retreat the day that video got leaked. As in, she couldn't have done it, because you're not allowed phones."

I pause again, thinking over what she said. There's no way that it couldn't have been Ally. All signs pointed to her, and she admitted it was her. "It was her, Tate. She confessed."

Tatum shrugs. "Ehhh, I just think that's Ally. She's going to take credit for any pain that has been inflicted on you, just because it's you. But I don't think she sent it."

"Well, maybe not." I drop my apple, appetite gone. "But she definitely had a part to play in it."

"Mmm," Tatum murmurs. "Which is my next thing. There's someone who was working with her if that's the case."

I look around the cafeteria, watching all the students,

in small cliques, some laughing, some drawing, some playing the guitar, and some just alone. "I haven't had any trouble from it since, so I don't want to look into it. Let's just drop it?"

Tatum nods. "Consider it dropped."

If she's right and someone was working with Ally, then there's someone here who is working against me. Could it be Lauren? But since Ally disappeared, she's been hanging around the nerd group.

Just as I'm about to open my mouth, Bishop walks into the cafeteria with the rest of the boys following closely behind. He takes a seat beside me, Nate sitting next to Tatum. I should really ask what's going on between the two of them, but I won't. I'm scared he's just using Tatum as a rebound from Tillie, because I saw how he was with Tillie. Without sounding completely bigheaded, I didn't even exist when Tillie was around, and since she's been gone, I can see, just slightly, not in an obvious way, what her absence has done to him. I know I was told not to look for her, but once all this shit is sorted with the Kings, and Daemon, and Katsia, and all the other things I've left out, if she's still not home, I will look for her.

Bishop wraps his arm around me, pulling me in and kissing me on the head. "Hey, baby."

Swoon.

I smile shyly. "Hey."

Tatum kicks me from under the table, so I look at her, widening my eyes to ask what the hell she wants. Her eyes shoot over her shoulder, so I follow, looking where she's pointedly staring, and that's when I see it. The whole school has pretty much stopped what they were doing to watch Bishop's and my exchange. It's unsettling and it's weird, but I've gotten used to it over the years. Not just because Bishop is who he is, but from always being the new girl. But attaining Bishop has made people's heads spin. He's the standoffish asshole. No one was good enough for him—until me.

"So, just a quick little question while I have everyone here. Carter is throwing a party this weekend to mark…." Tatum thinks over something and then shakes her head. "Never mind. I forgot what it was for, but anyway! I'm going. Mads?" She looks at me, her eyes wide like innocent little saucers. The innocence is a lie.

I stick my straw into my mouth. "Think I'll pass. I have a few things to do this weekend."

"Bishop being one of them?" she quips back, fluttering her eyelashes.

"Bishop being all of them," Bishop answers for me, picking me up from my seat and placing me onto his lap. I feel bad. I know I shouldn't, but I do. I know Tatum feels like she's losing her best friend since Bishop and I have been spending so much time together, and I don't want her to feel like that at all. Tatum's eyes drop to her food, and she picks at her orange.

Rolling my eyes, I turn to face Bishop. "Shall we go? Just for a little while. We don't have to stay late."

Bishop tosses one of my carrot sticks into his mouth and winks. "Yeah, babe." He looks over Tatum's shoulder, directly at Carter. "We should go." His eyes do that dark thing, and I spin back around, his hand gripping possessively on my thigh.

"We will come."

Tatum claps excitedly. "Yay, okay, so outfits—"

"Oh no." I cut her off. "Nope. You're on your own with that. I'll wear whatever I have."

Nate sits beside her, chatting to Eli and Brantley about

something, ignoring our entire conversation.

"Nate?" I question, waiting for him to answer.

"Yo?" He stops midconversation.

"Party at Carter's this weekend. You in?"

He looks to Bishop then slowly smirks. "Yeah, sounds good." Why do I feel like I've missed something? Why are they suddenly so interested to go to one of Carter's parties? Spinning back around to face Bishop, I see he's already staring at me when my eyes lock with his. I open my mouth, but he shakes his head, eating another carrot stick. "Later."

Giving him a small smile as a reply, I settle for it and turn back around. "So, outfits?" I grin at Tatum.

She wiggles her eyebrows. "Outfits."

"Jeans and a t—"

"More like skirts and G."

Bursting out laughing, I shake my head. "Oh, Tate."

CHAPTER 22

"I HATE YOU," I MUTTER TO TATUM. "I CAN'T BELIEVE you're making me wear this."

She laughs, walking out of the bathroom, spraying her Coco Chanel perfume all over herself. "Well, you know I know what's best for you. Like that dress—that dress is what's good for you."

I pick at the skirt. It's a tight, knee-length, black leather pencil skirt with a split that goes almost all the way up to my hip. She paired it with a thigh chain that dangles over my very exposed leg, and a little bralette crop top. Yes, the outfit is almost no outfit, and because the split is so high, I decided it was either a G-string or commando kind of night. Commando won. I slide on the nude lipstick and ruffle my hair into a nest of tousled mess. "Well," I mutter, slipping on some red pointy heels. Totally don't know how this is going to end, what with me in heels and everything, but again, that was Tatum being Tatum.

She snatches her bottle of vodka off the dresser. "Let's go. Is Sammy driving us?"

I nod. "Yeah, she's already waiting."

"And Bishop and Nate?" she asks, going for casual, but I see what she's doing.

"They'll meet us there, had something to take care of beforehand." I don't know what it was they had to take care of; I didn't care to ask. I respect there will be some things that Bishop can't tell me, especially when it comes to the Kings, so I won't pry for information unless it directly impacts me. Daemon still hasn't come out of his room, but I try every day. I knock, but he doesn't answer. I'm not sure what's going on with him, but all I know is I want to be there for him. Whatever it is he's going through.

Piling into the limo, Sammy gets into the driver seat and looks at me in the rearview mirror. "You be safe now."

"I'm always safe, Sammy."

She rolls her eyes. "Dressing like that is only asking for trouble."

"Just drive," Tatum says sassily to Sammy.

"Tate!" I growl her. "Shut up and drink."

She takes a sip and then passes it to me. "I don't want to get white girl wasted, but I'll have a little bit."

"Myth" by Tsar B starts playing, and I take a sip of the vodka, ignoring the way it stabs my throat when I swallow. "Sammy! Turn it up!" She does as she's told, winding up the window separator while she's at it. I give the bottle back to Tatum, and she scoots over beside me. "Oh! Selfie! Right

now." I move next to her and she snaps a hundred different selfies. All ranging from serious to duck face, to smiles,
laughing, to funny faces. I laugh, leaning back in my seat,
and look to Tatum. "I enjoy our friendship. You know that,
right?"

She waves me off. "Don't go soppy."

"I'm not!" I reply defensively. "Okay, maybe just a little,
but I just don't want you to feel left out now that Bishop and
I are...."

"Are...?" she prompts, an eyebrow raised. She must realize she's being a brat, because she rolls her eyes, her shoulders
dropping. "Look, okay, I'm just worried he's going to hurt
you." After drinking some vodka, she hands me the bottle.

"With good reason, but I don't think he will." I stare in
front of me, watching the tinted back window and the headlights of the car following us.

"What? So you're in love?" she asks.

I take a long pull of the vodka. Longer than I intended. I
really wasn't planning on getting drunk tonight, but with the
way this conversation is going, I'm going to be legless before
we even reach the party, and that will probably do all sorts
to piss off Bishop. Only because he's not there right now—I
don't think.

"I don't know. Love is a weird word."

"It's not a word, Mads." Tate looks at me, taking the vodka from me and bringing it to her lips. "It's a feeling."

"Well, I don't know what I'm feeling."

"Then it's love."

Turning my head, I look at her. "What do you mean?"

"It is what it is, Mads. You're in love with him, and for
that reason alone"—she shoves the vodka into me—"you're

going to need this a lot more than me."

I take it from her, taking another swig. "So you and Nate?"

She freezes then taps on the divider window. "Yo! Sammy! When are we there, homie?"

I laugh, fits of giggles erupting from my belly. She looks at me, pauses, and then starts laughing too. We're both swiping the tears from our eyes when the car stops outside of Carter's house, music blaring out and people already standing outside on his front porch drinking.

"Gah, I don't feel like going in now."

She laughs. "Just because you have a man to go home to, bitch. Come help me find my next victim."

"What?" I smirk as she opens her door. "You're not going to be in the room next to mine?"

She pauses then pushes open the door. "Okay, no, I won't be. I wanted something more, and he couldn't give it to me because apparently, he's into someone else. I can have him for sex only."

I step out of the car, thanking Sammy briefly and telling her I'd text her if we need a ride home. "You don't want that?"

She swallows, a sad look passing through her eyes. "With him? Unfortunately, not. I caught fucking feelings."

Hooking my arm with hers, I nudge my head toward the house. "Well, let's go get you a bed bud then!"

She grins, tilting the vodka up to her lips and swallowing. "Sounds brilliant."

Passing all the drunken people on the porch, I push open the front door just as my phone starts ringing in my little bag. I pull it out, blocking one ear to cut out the music, and search for a quiet corner to talk to Bishop.

"Bishop?" I yell into the phone, trying to drown out the music.

"Madison? Go home. Now!"

"What?" I can't hear his words properly; every time he says something, someone does something loud.

"Bishop?"

"Fuck!" he roars down the phone. I heard that.

"What did you say before?" Finally finding a bathroom, I close the door, the deep bass shaking through the walls.

"I can hear you now."

"Good. You need to leave right now. I'm on my way."

"What? Why?"

"Just fucking do it, Madison. For fuck's sake, I will kill you myself—"

Banging on the door interrupts. "Hang on. Wait there. Someone is knocking like they're the fucking five-oh."

"Madison!" he screams, just as I pull open the door.

"What the fu—" I pause, tilting my head. "Brantley?"

"Is that Bishop?"

I look down to my phone. "What? Yeah?"

"You can hang up. Come on, I'll get you out of here."

Swallowing past my distrust, I put the phone back into my bag, not hanging up. I've got scattered memories as a kid of Brantley and me, but I don't trust him. Every memory I have of him, which there is only one or two, it's clear he hates me. Even now, I see that he still hates me. Why though? I don't understand why he hates me.

"Madison?" Brantley pulls me into his side, his mouth coming to my ear. "There are some people here who are going to take you. I know you don't trust me, but you trust Bishop, who trusts me."

Wait!

"Wow! What?" I pause, just as we're about to get to the door. I look over my shoulder briefly, watching Tatum bump and grind up against some hottie to a techno song. How different our lives are going, like two different lanes. "I don't want…." I shake my head.

Brantley pulls open the front door and grips me around my arm, squeezing roughly. I look down at his grip and then look back to his face. "That's too hard."

"Shut the fuck up." We reach the end of the path just as a black limo pulls up, one much like ours. The back door swings open and Brantley grabs my hair, shoving me into the dark interior.

"Agh!" I scream, crawling to the corner of my chair.

Brantley gets in after, sitting beside me and unbuttoning his suit. "What the fuck?" I scream at him, but his eyes haven't moved. They're stationary, stuck on someone in front of him. When I follow his sight, I suck in a shocked breath. Not someone, someone*s.*

Bishop's dad, Hector, sits directly in front of me, and though I cannot see the man who is next to him due to the shadows cast over his spot, I see he's wearing a suit to match Hector's. "Um?" I clear my throat.

Hector just stares at me, fascinated. He's more than intimidating; he's downright lethal. He sucks the oxygen out of everyone sitting in the space. Now I see the apple doesn't fall far from the tree for Bishop.

He clears his throat. "You're quite the nuisance, Madison."

I look to Brantley, hate brewing in my gut. I trusted him; Bishop trusted him. That must be why Bishop told me to leave. I look back at Hector. "Wish I could say I was sorry."

Hector pauses, tilts his head, and then chuckles, pulling a cigar out from his suit jacket. "Well, I guess you have been reaping all the benefits."

"Why am I here?" I ask, sounding way more confident than I really am.

He rests his ankle on his knee, taking a puff of his cigar. "I thought it was about time you were filled in on something. A few things, actually."

"Oh?" I whisper out hoarsely. Secrets revealed just gives him more of a reason to kill me if he wants, but I'll take it.

"Does the name Venari mean anything to you, Madison?" His eye squints as the smoke puffs past.

Swallowing, I close my eyes, shutting out my early distant memories.

Don't remember.

Let it go.

Build the wall and stay over it.

"No." I open my eyes and plaster a fake smile. "It doesn't." Wall back up.

He narrows his eyes at me, as if to try to read my mind. He won't find anything by trying, just darkness and pain I've suppressed from childhood memories. Memories I used to fight every day to forget. But I'm curious how he knows that name. "Why?"

The limo stops and he looks to Brantley, gesturing toward the door. "Let's take a walk down memory lane."

He gets out of the car and I follow, shutting the door behind me. Walking around to the front of the car, the bright headlights beam up toward the log cabin.

Brantley steps up beside me as we both watch the front

door. "Bishop may be the king of the Kings, but he forgets there's a higher power than him. His dad."

I know this already, as I'm sure Bishop knows this too. Hector smiles at Brantley and pats him on the shoulder. "Good boy." Then I watch as he walks into the cabin.

"Brantley," I whisper. "What the fuck is going on here?"

He doesn't answer. He simply gestures toward the door, but it's not in an insolent way. His jaw is clenched, and there's fire in his eyes. He's not happy; actually, fuck that—he's pissed.

"I believe you already know who this is." Brantley puts a cigarette into his mouth and lights it, just as Hector steps down the cabin steps with—

I gasp, my legs turn to jelly, and my stomach recoils, breakfast threatening to come up.

Brantley's lip curls. "Daddy dearest, AKA—Lucan Vitiosus." Voices come in and out, my head pounding as memories start flooding back. All the hard work over the years I put into blocking them out doesn't mean shit now, because the wall hasn't just dropped. I look up, my eyes connecting with my childhood abuser, and that wall shatters to a million pieces. There's no rebuilding that.

Sucking in a shaky breath, I turn around and go to run, only someone steps in front of me, blocking me from going further, and I fall flat on my ass. That person isn't Brantley, because I see Black Converse shoes and tight yoga pants. I bring my eyes up to the small torso and frame until I'm met with one of the most exotic-looking girls I have ever seen in my entire life. Her black hair floats effortlessly and naturally down over her chest, her eyes curve in almonds, and her skin holds a natural golden tint. She's stunning in an obvious way. The kind of way that she'd gain attention anywhere she goes no matter what she's wearing. All that beauty gets washed out when she opens her mouth.

"You're so much prettier in photos." She tilts her head, and I stand to my feet, brushing off the dirt from my butt.

"Who the fuck are you?" I whisper out, I meant it to be harsher than it came out, but with tears pouring down my cheeks, I'm not in a very badass state right now.

Hector appears beside me and tsks. "Madison, play nice with Khales. She's a good little puppet."

I freeze. All thought processes mute, and my skin prickles to life. Khales?

I say the first thing that comes up in my head. "I thought you were dead."

She laughs, flicking her hair over her shoulder. "Naw, honey, there's so much"—she steps toward me and presses her finger to the tip of my nose—"you just don't know."

I step backward, squaring my shoulders. Is she intimating? Yes. But I've grown accustomed to being around a pack of wolves, so instead of running from them, I learned how to play with them. If she thinks I'm going to roll over and submit to her ways, she's deluded. Even if I'm feeling emotional about coming face-to-face with Lucan, I won't bow to her. "I don't doubt that at all, but why am I here?" I look to Hector. "Where is your son?"

Hector puts a cigar in his mouth. "He's not here." He lights the tip of the cigar and rolls it around in his mouth. The silence between all of us borders on awkward, so I turn around to focus all of my attention on Hector.

"And what exactly do you want with me? And why is she alive? Does Bishop know? Does anyone know? Why bring him out?" I point toward Lucan, the mere sight of him making my head spin and my hand itch. I think I've passed the shocked phase. I can feel myself slowly brewing, my anger like a swimming pool of lava at the bottom of a volcano, ready to erupt.

I look back to Khales. "And who *are* you, by the way?"

Hector shakes his head. "That's not important right now. What's important is this—"

"No." The word is instant and automatic.

"Oh?" Hector's eyebrows shoot up in surprise. "I see you've grown a little backbone now that you're not hiding behind my son."

I tilt my head and watch as the gray cloud of smoke floats into the dark night. "I never hid behind your son. He shielded me. There's a difference."

Hector leans back onto the car, and I step back a little so I can see both him, Khales, Brantley, and Lucan in my peripheral vision. "And anyway," I add, shooting a glare at Brantley, who is standing on the other side of the car. "Loyalty and all that—right, Brantley?"

"You don't know shit about loyalty," Khales murmurs, stepping up to me, chest-to-chest. I can feel her breathing labor as she looks down her nose at me.

I stand up straighter and match her stare. I don't know who I'm kidding; I've never been in a fight before, but I won't let someone hit me and get away with it. "You don't know shit about the shit I know, Khales, so step the fuck back."

"Okay, girls." Brantley grins, stepping between the two of us. "As much as this is getting my dick hard, we need to stay focused."

"You're disgusting," I mutter to Brantley, eyeing him up and down. I don't know what he's playing at or why he's here.

I'm not even 100 percent sure if he's on our side anymore.

"One question," I state, looking directly at Brantley. "Your birthday party, when we were little…."

Brantley's face drops. Hector remains quiet, watching me carefully.

"What of it?" Brantley asks, folding his arms in front of himself.

"What happened that day?" I whisper, leaning against the car. "I mean, I remember vague parts, but not all of it."

"So, what?" Brantley snarls. "You suddenly having memories and shit now?"

"No!" I snap back. "I just want to know why no one told me about this earlier."

Brantley looks to Hector, then to Lucan, who then looks to me.

Hector then looks to Lucan. "What birthday?"

My eyebrows pinch. "Wait!"

Brantley freezes.

Closing my eyes, I think back, digging for more from that day, but I was so young… so young.

"Where are we going?" I asked the man. He was the same man who hurt me at night. I didn't know why he hurt me, but he'd tell me not to tell any adults. I had to respect my elders, so I didn't tell a soul, afraid I'd get into trouble.

"You'll see, Silver," he murmured, his rough hand clutching onto mine as he pulled me down a long, dark hallway. We passed so many doors. All of them the color red. Not a nice red, a blood red. He stopped at a door, a door that had Vitiosus *on a gold plate hanging on the door. I looked up at the man, tilting my head. Over the time he hurt me, it would only ever be in my*

bedroom. *I didn't know why he had brought me here. To this place.*

He pushed open the door and gestured toward the room. "Go and get on the bed, Silver."

"No!" I scream, dropping to the ground. Shaking my head, I clutch my hair and pull at it, wanting to scratch the memories out of my head.

"Madison!" *Who is that?* It sounds like Bishop. "Brantley—"

Looking toward the bed, I swallowed, slowly stepping into the room. It was a big room. Gigantic. It was dim, almost dark in the room, and there was a big bed sitting to the side. I looked closer, stepping toward the bed, my heart beating in my chest and my throat clogged. All the lights were dim, but there was one shining on the bed, only when I got closer, I saw it was a camera sitting on a stand with a light pointing toward the mattress.

My eyebrows pulled together. "Wha—"

"Go to the bed, Silver." That voice. I hated that voice. I felt sick, my tummy not feeling good. Something was wrong, like it was always wrong when he was around. I hated him, but I obeyed because that was what I'd been told to do. I had to listen to adults; they always knew best. But why did he make me feel dirty? No other adult made me feel dirty. He made me sad, hurt, and angry all at once. I was confused, I think.

Walking toward the bed, I stopped at the foot of it. There was a small boy curled up on top of the covers, but he was wearing no clothes. Why was he wearing no clothes? He must've been cold.

"Silver, on the bed!" Lucan raised his voice at me, and I flinched, quickly crawling onto the soft mattress.

"Hi," I whispered out to the boy who was crying. "What's wrong?" I asked, wanting to know why he was so sad. Did he feel like I did? Did Lucan make him feel the same way I felt?

The boy sobbed then buried his head into the blanket. "Go away!" he yelled as he continued to cry. He was angry and sad, so maybe he did feel the same way as I did.

I stopped, sitting on the mattress as Lucan loosened his tie and pointed the camera at us. "Silver, take your clothes off."

"No!" I scream, sweat oozing out of my flesh. "Leave me alone. My name isn't Silver! It's Madison! Madison Montgomery! I'm not Silver!" I rock back and forth on the gravel road, trying to pull myself out of the memory.

"I—what about the boy?"

Lucan looked toward the boy on the bed, his lip curled. "Brantley, make room for Silver."

My eyes pop open and I shoot off the road, ignoring the tiny stones that are embedded into my flesh. "Brantley!" I scream.

Brantley turns to face me, a blank look pulling over his features.

I turn pale, all blood leaving my body. The pain, the anger, the sadness, it's all been cracked open again, and suddenly I'm that scared little girl again.

"What the fuck are they talking about?" Hector booms, losing his cool slightly. "And what the fuck just happened there, Madison?"

Headlights flash up the cabin, but I ignore them. I ignore everything.

And suddenly, rage. Pure rage electrifies me like a rush of adrenaline. Squaring my shoulders, I finally look directly at Lucan, the man who abused me as a child. The man my parents trusted. The man I thought I could trust. The man who made me keep secrets by using his "I'm an adult" card on me.

The man I want to kill.

"You!" I seethe.

His eyes join with mine, and he still looks the same, only older. So much older. His head is bald now, his face free of hair, but his eyes. His eyes will forever be the trigger to that feeling. That same feeling I felt when I was a little girl starts slowly slipping into me, but I fight it. I'm not her anymore. I'm older. More experienced. And though I may feel this pain for the coming months after being face-to-face with him, I know whatever I do it will be worth it. Car doors close in the distance behind me, but again, I ignore it. I ignore everything because my focus is solely on Lucan. Everything in my peripheral is closed.

I can hear people, or someone, walking toward us behind me, their feet crunching against the gravel, but I ignore it.

He chuckles. "Ain't no one gonna believe you, Silver."

The footsteps stop.

Ice cold wind whips my hair across my face, and that's when I know. I know those footsteps belong to Bishop and the Kings.

Lucan lunges at me, gripping my hair and pulling my back up against his front. It happens so fast I barely blink, but when I do, I see them. With my back pressed against Lucan's front, his gun pressing against my temple, I look pleadingly right at Bishop, but he's not looking at me. His shoulders are rising and falling in anger, his eyes zoned directly in on Lucan.

"What the fuck is going on here, son?" Hector asks calmly, not fazed I'm about to get my brains blown out everywhere. My heart pounds in my chest, and goose bumps prickle all over my flesh as fear ripples through me. No. There's no way. I didn't survive through all the memories, all the suppressed bullshit, only to go out by his hands. His hands already took so much from me; I won't let them take my life too.

Bishop steps forward, his lip curled and his eyes black. So black. I've not seen this look before; this is feral. Casting a look over his shoulder, Nate is there, the same position, his knuckles cracking. He starts jumping in his spot, craning his neck as if he's ready to fight. Which I have no doubt he is. The rest of the boys are there too, ready to throw down if they need to. Whether they know the story or not, I see it right there. Their loyalty to Bishop. It's unquestionable. This is The Elite Kings in full form.

"Ah!" Lucan presses the gun into my temple more. "Don't fucking move. Now, since people will be dying tonight, I want to get a few things out there for Silver so she knows the deal."

"Don't call me that," I hiss, my lip slightly curling.

"Hey, I'm doing you a favor."

"Fuck you."

He laughs, his breath falling over my neck. I can't hide the disgust; I dry heave, ready to spill my guts all over the road.

"What the fuck is going on?" Hector asks again.

Where is Brantley? This was all a setup. He and Khales

are nowhere to be seen. I look around again, as much as I can from the position I'm in, and sure enough, they're both not where they were a few minutes ago.

Hate.

"First, let me start with this. Silver, do you know much about the last names of these boys here?"

What?

"The hell has that got to do with you and what you did to me all those years ago?"

"I'll get to that part." He grins. I can hear it in his sick voice how much he's getting out of this, and that's the thing about age. The tone of your voice is one of the last things to change. Therefore, Lucan still has the same voice.

"What are you doing, Lucan?" Hector warns. His tone should be enough to put the fear of God into Lucan, but it doesn't, because he continues.

"Hector and Bishop Hayes... Hayes meaning 'The Devil,'" he starts, and just as I open my mouth to ask another question, his hand slams over it, pausing me. "Everyone shut the fuck up and let me finish, or I swear to God I will shoot her."

He clears his throat, before smugly murmuring, "Now, where was I? Oh yes, the names. Lucan and Brantley Vitiosus. I'll get to the meanings of the names and the English translations when I've finished." He laughs. Then his lips skim over my earlobe before he whispers, "and you know how theatrical I can get, don't ya, Silver?"

The first teardrops, followed by anger. Rage.

He continues. "Max, Saint, and Cash Ditio. Phoenix and Chase Divitae. Raguel, Ace, and Eli Rebellis." He laughs at these last two. My eyes shoot toward Nate, who is now being held back by Chase and Cash. He looks absolutely feral.

The lack of light and smudged tears in my eyes make for hard looking, but even if I couldn't see it, I could sure as fuck feel it.

Lucan carries on. "Nate *Malum*-Riverside." Then he laughs, bringing his lips to my ear again.

I shut my eyes, fighting the bile that's about to spew out of my mouth from not just his proximity, but his touch. "Johan, Hunter, Jase, and Madison *Venari*."

I freeze. All life drains from my face.

"You hear that, Silver? You're adopted... you and that skitzo brother of yours."

What? More tears spill out of my eyes. This can't be true. There's no way. He's fucking with me. My dad is my dad and my mom was my mom. Lucan is being what he is.

I look at Bishop, who is finally looking directly at me, and I see it. The look. It's the look he gives me when it's just us together. His eyebrows are furrowed and his eyes are zeroed into mine.

Not only is it true, but he knew.

Sobs wrack through my body, and my knees buckle, but Lucan yanks me back up. "Careful, careful... maybe you can talk with your man here about the meanings of those last names and what they mean in regards to each family's duty in The Kings, but let me tell you this, Silver," he whispers so harshly into my ear. "When you know all there is to know about this—they will kill you."

I don't care.

I'm adopted. My whole life was a lie. I was wrong. I can't trust anyone. I can only trust Daemon. *Daemon*. His face lights up inside my head, but instead of it soothing me, it brings on another set of tears.

"So I'll make this easier for you and tell you the big fire-work kicker!" he yells, laughing hysterically. Leaning down, I pause, my heavy breathing the only thing breaking the silence.

"You—"

A gun fires and Lucan screams, his hand loosening from around my mouth as he falls to the ground.

I freeze, static buzzing in my ears from the gunshot.

Pain.

Anger.

Rage.

Rage.

Rage.

Heat rises inside of me as I think over everything. His touch when I was a kid. What he made me do to Brantley. And what he made Brantley do to me as a kid.

"Stop!" I scream, my eyes unblinking and fixed on the car in front of me.

Silence.

I slowly turn around, noticing Bishop is beside me, kneeling down next to Lucan, who is bleeding out on the road.

I look at Lucan, tilting my head. Smiling, I whisper out, "Seeing you in pain soothes my anger."

Lucan looks at me square in the eye. "I will live in your memories, Silver. Forever."

Squaring my jaw, I bend down to Bishop's level, bringing my hand to his boot. I feel up toward where I know he keeps a knife. I feel him freeze, realizing what I'm about to do, but before he can stop me—if he was going to stop me—I unclip the holster and pull out the large hunting knife then slowly raise it into the air. Lucan's eyes follow it slowly.

"You see this?" I run my pointer finger down the blunt side of the knife. "It's a Fallkniven A1Pro Survival Knife." I smirk, admiring how the boys—except for Bishop, he's still crouching beside me—watch me with awe, or fear, or a combination of both, and are all standing behind me. They have my back—but I won't need it. I launch the knife into Lucan's pelvis area until I feel his bones crunching against the blade. He screams out, a loud, curdling scream, his back arching and tears pouring down his face.

I bend down to his ear, running my lips over the lobe like he did to me not long ago. Feeling his blood spilling over my hand, I grin and whisper, "You know, since you love to be theatrical... this knife is a survival knife." I circle the blade, my hand sticky from his blood. It blankets my anger, soothing it like an ice pack on a burn. Putting out the pain.

Pulling the knife out from him, I inch backward, both hands wrapped around the blade, ready to stab it into his head. Needing it to finally put out the burn I have inside me. The burn has only been temporarily eased, when Brantley appears, snatches the knife out of my hand, and stabs it right between Lucan's eyes. Blood sprays out all over me, the tang of blood overpowering every taste bud in my mouth.

Brantley screams, veins popping out from his neck, his eyeballs almost bulging from their sockets. He has anger; I was right. He has anger just like I did, if not more, because Lucan was his father.

My breathing slows, and when Lucan's head drops to the side, his death stinking up the air, I collapse into Bishop, my head resting on his shoulder.

He wraps his arm around me, kissing me on the head, as Brantley pulls the knife out of his dad and launches it back into him again. And again. And again. I flinch, digging my face into Bishop. His smell, his just—Bishop. The only sound I can hear is Brantley slicing into Lucan. Again and again.

"Come on, baby," Bishop says into my hair when he sees Brantley isn't stopping anytime soon.

"Well," Hector says, and I turn in Bishop's grip to face him but away from Brantley making dues with his abusive dad. "This is all lovely, but do any of you fuckers want to tell me what the fuck is going on and why my right-hand man is dead? Brantley, hear that? He's dead so you can stop that now." Hector pauses, looking at the mess Brantley has created, and then shrugs like he sees that type of shit daily. He probably does. Actually, all of them seem unbothered by it.

Bishop squeezes me into him. "Lucan would rape Madison when she was a little girl."

Hector sucks from his cigar, but just there, below the surface, I can see it enrages him somewhat, and that surprises me because he's Hector Hayes. I wouldn't think something like that would bother him. He must catch my notice in him, because he laughs.

"Don't take it to heart, sugar. I personally don't like you, for a lot of reasons." He looks at his son and then back to me. "But I don't condone rape."

"And…" Bishop pauses but then continues. "…and Brantley."

The stabbing sound has stopped; now it's sobbing. Not the quiet sobbing, it's the ugly kind, and I turn in Bishop's embrace, finally bracing myself to look toward Brantley.

He has his arms wrapped around his knees and is rocking beside what is left of Lucan. Blood drips from his hair, face, and hands, but he just rocks, sobbing loudly. "I didn't want to. Why? Why did you have to make me do it? All those times…." He shakes his head. My heart snaps. I slowly start to walk toward him, when Bishop grabs onto my arm.

I turn to face him, and he shakes his head. "Don't."

"What do you mean, don't? No wonder he hates me, Bishop," I whisper, searching Bishop's eyes. "He needed someone to blame, so he blamed me for what his father made us do that day. He blamed me, because if I didn't exist, that wouldn't have happened."

Bishop shakes his head. "No, babe." But then his eyes go over my shoulder.

"Thirty-seven," Brantley whispers from behind me, and I quickly spin around to face him. "Thirty-seven young girls."

What? I want to ask, but I don't in fear that he might snap at me. Instead, I remain silent, hoping he will say more, which he does.

He looks at me, the headlights from the car shining on his face now that he's level with it. Blood paints his face and clothing, the knife gripped in his hand. He tosses the knife over and it lands near Bishop's feet. "You're right though," he starts, sidestepping around the mangled corpse on the ground. "I hated you. I never understood why you came back. When we were kids, at my birthday party, I hated all kids, not just you, but my father had already started talking about what he was going to get us to do together." He pauses. "When you started Riverside, I didn't know at first whether you remembered me or not. At first, I thought you did remember and you were—I don't know—fucking with us after some revenge for what Lucan did." Shit, that makes a whole lot of sense. "But also…" He pulls out a pack of smokes and puts one into his mouth, lighting it. "…you were my first. So there was hate for you from that as well. I didn't make the Silver connection to The Silver Swan, which I should have. I'm an idiot for not making that connection. I just figured it was because of your eyes. They're murky green now, but when you were a kid, they were silver."

I nod, because they were. It was always strange.

He steps up to me, leaving the smoke in his mouth. "Do you feel that?" he asks, tilting his head.

I look deep into his eyes, a sense of peace washing over me. The fire I had burning for so many years from undying hate toward Lucan had gone out. Smiling, I nod. "Yeah."

He blows out a cloud of smoke. "At least that's one of us." He narrows his eyes at me.

I frown. "You still hate me?"

His eyebrows shoot up in surprise. "No, fuck." His eyes dart around the place. "It's just—never mind. But I don't hate you. I feel peace with *you* now." Then he smiles. The first time I have ever seen Brantley smile, and it's at me. I want to jump on him and hug him, but that's probably going too fast for him. Baby steps.

Turning back around, wrapping my arms around Bishop, I look over his shoulder, directly at Hunter and Jase. My brothers. Biological brothers with Daemon.

Hunter steps backward, shaking his head and walking straight toward the parked car, slamming the door behind him. I frown, my shoulders dropping. I don't know what I expected, but it wasn't for Hunter to act like that. He's always been warm toward me.

Jase just stares at me, his dark eyes glued to mine. The last string in my heart is about to snap when he smiles at me. Giving me a wink. For the older brother, that surprises me. I haven't spent much time with Jase, if any, but I know in that moment that will change.

Bishop tucks me under his arm as the rest of the boys walk back to the cars. He looks at his dad. "Want me to call Katsia about this mess, or do you want to?" he asks his dad, nudging his head toward the destruction on the road.

Hector looks at me and then looks at Bishop. "I'll call her." Then he looks to me. "There was a reason for my bringing you here tonight, and it wasn't that."

I sink into Bishop, and his grip tightens around me. "Though, I did plan to tell you that you're adopted." He looks to Bishop. "But you see, as much as I love my son, he did something bad tonight. Something that is against our rules. And we only have one rule, Madison." Hector looks right at me, and chills break out over my flesh. "So now that your adoption is exposed, I guess it's only fair I find something else to tell you since my son is so trigger happy tonight."

I look up at Bishop. Trigger happy?

Hector steps forward, pushing his hands into his pockets. "I'm sure you're familiar with the initiation process of a King?" he questions, looking at me. I nod. "Very good. So you know..." He gestures behind him, and Khales reemerges from the shadows. Bishop freezes, his grip turning to steel. "...that Khales was Bishop's..." My head spins and my stomach recoils. Someone else steps out of the shadows. "...as was your adopted 'mother.'"

The End

Tacet a Mortuis (Whispers from the Dead), the final book told from Madison, and now, Bishop, coming soon.

ACKNOWLEDGEMENTS

I just want to thank everyone who has helped contribute to not only my stories, but to my sanity. Don't all laugh at once!

First of all, my children and partner. They're my rock, my home, my loves, and my most favorite people walking this earth. Everything I do, I do for them.

I want to thank my family who continues to support me.

Isis! My best bitch. Somewhere between a sister and a soul mate. You've been my #1 supporter, counselor, therapist, just basically my all-around PERSON. You're *my* person.

My Wolf Pack! You girls keep me going even on my darkest of days. You make me smile when I want to frown—this is getting soppy… oh look! The D…

My betas, thank you for reading my unedited words. Truly, you probably deserve a medal or something.

Kayla for editing my words! The girls from Give Me Books for handling all my promo, Jay Aheer for always getting my covers on point. And Champagne Formatting for making the words all laid out nicely.

Thank you to my author buds who always keep it real! Nina Levine, River Savage, Chantal Fernando for the epic sprint sessions and our meme shares, Leigh Shen, Anne Malcom, Addison Jane. You girls are rad, got mad love for all of you.

Made in the USA
Columbia, SC
10 June 2021